Kit Morgan is Brokenhead's sex therapist by day and Dominatrix by night. While she never shies away from being her true self, she rarely mixes business with pleasure until she meets Greg Anderson, the owner of the only two horses in this kinky two-horse town.

Submissive Greg longs to turn his ranch into a BDSM bed and breakfast—a safe place to stay and play for those in the kink lifestyle. He's looking for a partner in life and business, and he wonders if he's found that in Kit.

Will they ride off into the sunset, or tie each other up in knots?

Roping the Rancher
Copyright © 2019 Kellie Kamryn
ISBN: 978-1-4874-2669-9
Cover art by Martine Jardin

Published by eXtasy Books Inc or
Devine Destinies, an imprint of eXtasy Books Inc

Look for us online at:
www.eXtasybooks.com or www.devinedestinies.com

Roping the Rancher
Brokenhead Hearts Book 2

By

Kellie Kamryn

CHAPTER ONE

K it Morgan bit her lips together, brushed back a lock of dark hair behind one ear, closed the notebook she held in one hand, and set it down on the table in front of her beside a tissue box. She leaned over and took the hands of the elderly woman in front of her.

Although the term *elderly* didn't describe Trudy Anderson in the least. Well into her late sixties, the woman had more energy than women half her age and talked a mile a minute.

Currently, Trudy's silver head bobbed as her plump body shook with sobs. Kit squeezed her hands and tried hard not to roll her eyes. She'd never known someone who could turn the waterworks on and off as fast as this woman.

Kit massaged the back of one of Trudy's hands, hoping to soothe her. "There, there . . . It will be all right."

Trudy hiccupped, then let loose another barrage of sobs. "It . . . will . . . never . . . be . . . all . . . right . . ."

It took effort for Kit to refrain from heaving a sigh. *She's pouring it on thick today.* "Your son, Greg, is a grown man, Trudy. He is capable of making his own decisions. You can't force someone to seek counselling if they don't want it."

Trudy lifted her head, beseeching Kit with wide tear-filled grey-blue eyes.

Kit had to work at keeping her facial expression neutral. During another session, Trudy had pleaded with Kit to counsel her son. Kit had insisted Greg make his own appointment if he felt he needed it. She'd figured Trudy would bring it up again at some point, but she hadn't expected the woman to resort to tears on the matter.

Kit kept her tone gentle. "Mrs. Anderson—Trudy—it sounds like Greg is coping just fine. You've told me time and again how he's always felt at home on the farm, so it would not be unusual for him to throw himself into working on the property to cope with his loss. Everyone grieves in their own way in their own time. Not everyone requires counselling, and certainly not the kind I provide."

Teardrops dripped down Trudy's face, and she opened her mouth to protest. Kit held up a hand to stop her. *The woman should win an Oscar.* "Trudy, I want to focus on you. It's why you're here."

The tears ceased as abruptly as they'd started. Trudy slipped her hands away from Kit and wiped the tears from her face. "Well, I had to try."

Kit shook her head, and another strand of dark hair escaped her bun. She tucked it back behind her ear and suppressed a chuckle. "You're a good woman and a great mother."

Trudy sighed and shrugged. "Not according to him. I never know what is going on in his life. I figured you'd help an old lady."

"You're hardly old." Kit sat back in her chair. "An award-winning performance. Nice try milking it for all it's worth."

Trudy sighed again and reached for a tissue. A honking sound emanated from her nose, and Kit waited for her to finish. As Trudy disposed of the tissue in the garbage can to the right of the table, she said, "I want him to be happy. He rarely smiles, and he works all the time. That cannot be healthy."

"What is healthy for one individual might be harmful to another. Only a therapist would be able to determine that." Kit picked up the notebook and consulted her notes.

"That's why I wanted him to see you."

"I'm not a grief counsellor," Kit reminded her. "I'm uncertain Greg needs the services I provide."

"You said it yourself, *people grieve in their own way.* Maybe

2

he needs some sex therapy."

"That's hardly for you to decide. And I cannot help people if they don't want it." Kit cleared her throat, trying not to picture the tall, dark, and handsome rancher she'd had the pleasure of being intimate with. She had left out that bit of information when Trudy had first made her plea. As a therapist, she believed all information should be confidential, especially personal information.

Kit wanted to get to know Greg better, but in a personal way, and not as a counsellor, and most definitely not because his mother had set them up. "So, you said he wants to open a bed and breakfast on the farm?"

Trudy beamed, nodding with enthusiasm. "That's right. I'm so proud of him. He wants to own his own business and generate more tourism for the town."

"Sounds like he has his hands full." Kit tilted her head with a nod. "Let's talk about that. How does it make you feel?"

"Oh, I'm sure whatever he's doing keeps him busy. I worry about him being all alone out there. He needs people. We all need people. And he hasn't spoken to me about his father's death. In fact, we don't talk much at all. Haven't since he was a boy."

"You've mentioned that before. What happened between the two of you?" Kit picked up a pencil, tapping the eraser against her chin.

Trudy lifted her hands in the air. "I don't know. He was a talkative child and then stopped one day. Since then, I always do the talking, and he listens. He never confides in me about anything."

Kit understood Trudy's concern for her son, but she didn't feel there was any reason to worry. A grown man, Greg probably realized, as most of the town did, that big-hearted Trudy was the biggest gossip around. She knew everybody's business, and Greg had most likely clammed up at some point to keep his business private. Kit had a sneaking suspicion as to why.

Trudy heaved a dramatic sigh and threw herself back into the couch. "If I die, then he'll have no one. It's a mother's worst nightmare."

Kit coughed to suppress a giggle. "If you're dead, you won't be able to worry about him anymore. Problem solved."

Trudy narrowed her eyes. "You really have a way of getting right to the point."

Kit shrugged a shoulder. "One of my instructors used to say I had a way of cutting through bullshit."

"What?" Trudy squawked. "Are you saying I'm full of shit?"

"Of course not. I'm saying I have a knack for getting to the heart of the matter. And I want to concentrate on why you're here, not the fact your son won't come for counselling."

"You keep asking about him. And he needs it in my opinion." Trudy crossed her arms over her chest and huffed. "He's thirty-three years old, and I don't know if he's ever had sex. He's never introduced me to any woman."

"People like their privacy, and often from family," Kit pointed out.

Trudy sat up and leaned forward, glaring at her. "Are you saying my son would keep things from me on purpose?"

Yes. Yes, I am. Kit cleared her throat once more. "No, that's not what I'm saying. What I'm trying to say is that sometimes people need to do things in their own time, and when your son finds a partner he wants to spend his life with, I'm sure he'll let you know."

Trudy frowned, real tears forming this time.

Kit reached across the table and took her hand again. "I know you're worried about Greg because he used to confide in your late husband. Then Walter would fill you in. Without Walter, you feel lost about your son's life. In my opinion, the two of you either need to find a way to communicate, or else consider it's time you both moved on and accept your relationship as it is. It's not unhealthy for parents and children to grow apart and have separate lives."

"I suppose," Trudy capitulated. "But if he were to make an appointment, you'd see him, right?"

Kit sat back and nodded. "Yes, of course. If Greg chose to come in, I would speak with him."

Trudy's eyes lit up.

Kit knew exactly where she'd try to go next. She cut her off at the pass. "Trudy, anything Greg confides in me is confidential. I cannot report to you on your son's life."

The hope in Trudy's eyes deflated. "Rats."

Kit inhaled a deep breath. She loved helping her clients, but Trudy was another breed altogether. "Let's talk about something else. How did your date go?"

Trudy waved a hand. "It went all right. Ed had trouble keeping it up, but we eventually got his pecker to work."

Kit swallowed a laugh, picked up her notebook, and jotted a note. "Were you satisfied with the experience?"

"Well . . ." Trudy sighed. "He's no Walter, and he'll need some serious instruction on eating pussy, but I think we can figure things out. If not, Doug in apartment four has been giving me the eye for the last few days."

"So, you feel you might not want an exclusive relationship?"

"I don't know." Trudy shrugged. "At my age, I don't want to be alone. I have to admit, though, I love being pursued by more than one man."

Kit smiled. "That is exciting. Must make you feel good. And multiple partners can work if everyone communicates and is on the same page about what they want and desire."

"You know about that, eh?"

"I do indeed." Kit had never hidden her bisexual nature

from anyone in town, nor had she hidden any of her relationships.

"That's what I like about you—not afraid to be yourself."

"Thank you. And I admire you for the same." Kit nodded with a smile.

Trudy beamed. "Yeah, I do feel good. When I first moved into Shady Oaks, I wondered who would want an old cunt like me, but it turns out that half the male population there wants a piece of this ass." She leaned to one side and slapped her rear. "Helps that the female to male ratio is on the low side."

Kit bit her lower lip to keep her laughter in check. Trudy's colourful commentary made for great file notes. "How do you feel I can help you now that you've gotten back in the saddle, so to speak?"

"I like talking to you, sharing it with you. Like a girlfriend I pay to be my friend." Trudy chuckled. "Someone to tell my troubles to, someone to give me sex tips."

"Well, that I can do, and I'm happy to help." Kit glanced at the clock on the wall. "It seems our time is up for the day. Keep up the good work of communicating with your suitors. Communication is key in any relationship. You know your body, so teach them how to use it."

Trudy pushed herself to a stand. "You got it, sister."

Kit stood and walked Trudy to the door.

Trudy turned and gave her a quick hug. "You'll be at the bake sale on Saturday?"

"If you're baking your chocolate chip cookies and coconut pies, you bet your darned patootie I'll be there." Kit winked.

"Girl, ya gotta lay off the old people talk. Add a few f-bombs once in a while." Trudy chucked her on the chin. "Thanks for the talk today."

"A pleasure to help, as always." Kit held the door open.

"Oh, and pencil me in for next Wednesday," Trudy called

over her shoulder. "I've got another hot date this Saturday night, and I want to tell you all about it."

"Wednesday it is. I'll add it to my appointment book. Have a good day, Trudy."

"You too, counsellor." Trudy saluted and continued down the sidewalk into the sunshine.

Kit closed the door, marvelling at the session. If she didn't know better, she'd think Trudy was trying to set her up with her son. The thought of Greg sent a shiver of pleasure up her spine.

Kit shook her head and tidied up the small office to get ready for her next client. She counselled a lot of people in the small town of Brokenhead—regarding their sex lives. Despite knowing intimate details about so many individuals, gossip didn't abound. She had a strict confidentiality policy, and everyone respected how much she helped them with their relationships.

On occasion, a few of the kinkier people who lived in the area hired her as a professional Domme. Sex was never part of her contracts, but she helped couples learn about BDSM and provided services for individuals who wanted to investigate the lifestyle or experience particular kinks.

She'd had a string of lovers back when she lived in the city, but since moving to Brokenhead full time, her best friend, Kat Monroe, had been her only constant. Both bisexual, they were lovers on occasion and shared a deep emotional relationship.

A few months ago, Kat had begun dating the local vet, Evan Cole. They'd been intimate ever since, but Evan had been open to sharing Kat for the occasional threesome. Kit was happy her best friend had found a relationship that would allow her to be her true self and not keep her away from people who were important to her.

A twinge of jealousy pinched Kit's heart, but she rubbed it away. She had wanted a partner to do life with for as long as she could remember, but she hadn't found the right person yet.

When Greg Anderson had approached her about a business arrangement, they'd spent all night talking logistics. He was tall and handsome, with a lean muscled bod, short brown hair, and into BDSM, and Kit wondered if she'd found her match. Greg, a submissive, seemed perfect for her Domme side. After their encounter had become personal, he'd shied away from speaking to her at all.

Kit sighed. She understood Trudy's frustration with her son. Despite Kit's best efforts, she hadn't been able to get Greg to open up to her again. She didn't want to give up, yet she didn't want to compromise her integrity either. Plus, she didn't know if she could have a business-only relationship with Greg after their intimate time together.

The rugged, rigid rancher kept to himself, and she knew she couldn't make him speak to her if he didn't want to.

Kit walked over to the desk and checked her appointment book for her next client. The next person wouldn't arrive for almost an hour. She smiled and reached back to let her hair down from its bun. Her dark locks cascaded down her shoulders, and she shook her head from side to side. She opened the door that led to the basement and descended the stairs. Now, what outfit to wear for the client who wanted a good spanking?

Greg closed the stall door and wiped the sweat from his brow. One of his mares hadn't been feeling well, but she seemed okay now. Thanks to his buddy, Evan, she'd perked up considerably since she'd shit herself and ruined Evan's date.

The sound of a car engine caught his attention, and he sighed. *Ah, mother . . . Now what do you want?*

He removed the cowboy hat from his head, scratching his

scalp until he winced. Then he grabbed a fistful of hair and tugged. The pain shot through his body, relaxing him. Whenever he needed a reprieve or to relax, he'd do something that caused a little physical discomfort. Nothing close to self-harming, but he'd learned long ago that a small jolt of pain to his system triggered a relaxing sensation afterward. Learning this about himself had led to his interest in BDSM.

Greg inhaled another deep breath, then exhaled slowly, counting to ten. He closed his eyes and concentrated on the sound of his mother's approach — the slam of the car door, her calling his name, the crunch of gravel as her footsteps brought her nearer to the barn. For a brief moment, he contemplated hiding in one of the stalls, but the animals might give away his presence. Besides, no matter how annoyed he could be with her, he would never hide from her for long.

While he and his mother hadn't been close since he was a boy, he loved his mother with all his heart. He'd never known how to talk to her, too afraid her gossipy ways would make his business town news. Shy and reserved, he had always cringed at Trudy's larger than life personality that didn't mesh with his.

His dad had sat down with him one day and told him that, if he felt comfortable, Greg could confide anything to him and he'd only reveal as little information as possible to satisfy his mother's desire to know he was all right. Greg had trusted his dad, and he'd never let him down. His mother had never nagged Greg for personal information, and the three of them had co-existed peacefully for all his teen and adult years.

Sadness welled up inside. With his father gone six months now, the divide between him and his mother seemed a chasm too big to bridge, and he didn't know if he could trust her to keep his secrets. He wasn't even sure if he wanted to reveal anything more of himself to her than she already knew. And while his heart ached for his dad, he still had a parent, alive and well, who cared for him. He needed to figure out a way to have a relationship with his mom before it was too late.

"In here, Mom!" Greg called out, and within a few seconds, Trudy poked her head around the barn door.

"There you are." Trudy beamed from ear to ear.

Greg couldn't help but smile at his mother. Despite what he saw as her flaws, she had a heart of gold, and he loved her dearly.

He placed the hat back onto his head, peeled off his leather work gloves, put them on the table beside him, and held open his arms. His mom, wearing her signature floral over-long shirt—to cover her ample frame—with black tights and two-inch heels, clicked her way across the wood floor to him for a hug. She burrowed her head under his chin and squeezed him tight.

After a brief embrace, she tipped her head back, and her silver pixie-cropped hair tickled his chin. She stared up at him, concern crinkling her brow.

Greg kissed her forehead, then held her away at arm's length. "Don't start, Mom. I eat just fine, I'm not too thin, I don't work too hard, and I don't need time off."

Trudy's mouth gaped open like a fish out of water for a few seconds. Then she snapped it closed and stepped back with her hands on her hips. "Well, what am I supposed to talk to you about then?"

He smiled. "Anything else."

"Well . . . Well . . ." Trudy stuttered, her gaze travelling around the barn. "How's Momma doing?" She gestured toward the horse who had been under the weather.

Greg nodded, wondering if maybe he'd underestimated his mother all these years. After all, anything he'd told her, she remembered. "She seems to be doing better."

"Well, that's good. It would be a shame for you to lose revenue due to a sick animal," she said. "Did the doc ask for a reimbursement?"

He shook his head, marvelling at the fact she'd remembered that he'd rented the mare to his friend for a romantic horse and carriage ride. "No, Evan didn't ask. I gave him a discount, and he's only charging me for the meds she needs. He's a good friend."

Trudy flashed him a quick smile, then frowned in the direction of the horse. "I don't know why you had to name her after me. I am not fussy or ornery."

Greg stifled a laugh. "That's not why I named her Momma."

She gave him a look that said she believed otherwise.

Greg shook his head again, slung an arm around her shoulders, and kissed the top of her head. "She works hard and shows her personality. Just like the mom I know and love."

She snorted. "Oh, please. She's always been picky about what she eats and particular about the amount of hay in her stall, and she likes being brushed in a certain way." She wagged a finger at him and pushed from his embrace. "Don't think I don't know how you really feel about your mother."

Greg rolled his eyes. "I love you, Mom. You know that. And you don't have to cause tension to have a conversation with me."

Trudy stomped her foot and glared like a petulant child. "I'm not causing tension."

He raised an eyebrow.

She deflated. "I don't know how else to talk to you."

The sincere tone in her voice poked at his heart. "Without Dad around, maybe it's time we learned."

She blinked at him for a second or two, a surprised expression on her face.

He folded his arms across his chest, then raised a finger. "All I ask is no nagging. You can ask questions, but accept it if I don't wish to answer."

Her lower lip wobbled, and tears formed in her eyes.

He hadn't meant to make her cry. "Mom, I'm sorry if . . . Oof!" He stumbled back when she rushed into his arms.

He held her tight, rocking her back and forth and recalling how she'd done the same for him when he was a boy. *Oh, how times change . . .*

Trudy looked up, mascara tear-tracks running down her face. "Oh, that would be wonderful."

He smiled and shrugged. "It's a start."

Her tears dried up, and she brushed the backs of her hands over her cheeks. "And I have one thing to ask of you."

Taken aback at her sudden change in demeanour, he responded with caution. "What would that be?"

"I'd like you to come to counselling with me next week."

He narrowed his eyes. "Why?"

"I have something I'd like to share with you, but I would like Kit's support when I do. It's the only time I'll ask, I promise."

"I thought Kit was a sex therapist?"

"She is."

He studied her for a second and shook his head. "I don't want to know about your sex life, Mom."

"She and I talk about more than sex. Please?"

Greg sighed and held up a finger. "Just once?"

Trudy nodded.

The thought of seeing Kit caused heat to rush through his body. Maybe it wouldn't hurt to see Kit in a controlled environment. He kissed his mom's forehead. And if it helped build a bridge between him and his mom, he would go. "You've got a deal."

"Great. What are you doing for dinner?" his mom asked.

"I'll be eating whatever you make," he teased, glad she'd changed the subject.

"Then I'll go see what you've got in your fridge to work

with." Trudy clapped her hands together and sashayed from the barn.

Greg shook his head. He knew he'd used his dad as a buffer between him and his mom for years, but with his dad gone, he needed to forge a relationship with his mother they could both live with. And he knew his dad would be proud of that.

He sauntered toward the house after his mother. A length of rope hanging on the wall caught his eye, and a rush of excitement coursed through him. He took hold of the end of the rope and rolled up the end of one shirt sleeve. Brushing the length across his forearm sent a shiver of delight down his spine. He wound the end around his bare forearm in a slow, deliberate manner. Then he tightened the length, pain biting into his skin. Euphoria replaced the sting.

He sighed in contentment and loosened the binding from his arm. He'd been experimenting with self-tying for years, researching on the internet and in books. A few years back, he'd attended a Shibari convention out of town, and allowed himself to be tied up for all to see. It had felt freeing to be amongst people where he could be himself.

It had taken him some time to come to terms with his submissive nature, to see that it didn't lessen his manhood to surrender to his needs. He enjoyed the kind of pain that brought pleasure and the relaxation that came with bondage for him — sometimes at another's mercy. But he had yet to find a permanent play partner. While he knew a traditional monogamous relationship wasn't for him, he wanted a Domme he could count on, someone to build with.

Kit. His brain whispered her name to him again. He'd known for some time that she was the local Dominatrix, but when he had approached her a few months ago, it was about a business arrangement. With her knowledge and expertise, he figured she could run all sorts of workshops for people out at the ranch. He wanted to turn the farm into a bed and breakfast that served as a BDSM playground and safe place for people to explore their kinky side.

Greg shivered remembering the night he'd invited her over to discuss his plans and show her one of the barns he'd been converting into a playhouse. Kit had been almost as excited as he over everything. He'd gotten caught up in the excitement of the moment and revealed his personal inclinations toward pain and bondage. Kit had asked if she could tie him up to practice her rope skill. He'd agreed to submit, and once she'd tied him up, he'd begged her to spank him. After a short discussion, Kit complied, and the experience had been euphoric for him. In fact, he'd climaxed at the end of their session.

Stunned at the experience, and how easy it had been to be with Kit, he'd avoided her since. The last time he'd seen her, he'd gone over to the house she shared with her roommate, Kat, to rescue his sick horse from the disaster of a date Evan had tried to put together for Kat.

When a male friend had stopped by to see Kit, Greg had been reminded of the numerous people in town who must know Kit in intimate ways. His ego had taken a hit, and he'd put up a wall. Surely someone as vivacious as her would never be interested in him. And his brain had been calling him a coward ever since.

Greg blew out a breath and hung the rope back on the hook. He'd always been a homebody, never wanting to leave Brokenhead permanently. He'd always loved the farm and had dreamed of one day owning the place so he could turn it into his personal pleasure paradise where he and others from all over the world could meet and play. With his dad now passed, and the property in his name, Greg felt his dream was much closer to reality.

An image of Kit's oval face, framed by dark hair, swam into view. He sighed, picturing her dark eyes sparkling with kindness and caring, much the way they had when she'd looped a piece of leather around his neck and tugged his face to hers. His body shuddered in remembrance of the occasion and the knowledge he'd felt safe with her.

He shook his head to clear the image. Kit was the only other person in town who would fully support his idea of a safe place for kinksters on the grand scale he imagined. He knew she would be the perfect person to help him achieve his goals. He just needed to get out of his own way to be able to work with her.

Well, I have an appointment with her next week. He'd never been great at communicating with women. Better late than never to start. *How hard could it be?*

CHAPTER TWO

At the sound of the knock on the door, Kit rose from her desk and smoothed down her pencil skirt. *Gotta give Trudy credit, the woman is never late.*

Kit glanced down at her desk, eyeing the half-eaten cookie lying on the plastic wrap. She smiled at the other thing she could count on from Trudy — her impeccable baking. Kit was always first in line at community bake sales for Trudy's goodies, and she had a hard time not scarfing down the delectable treats whenever she had the opportunity to get her hands on them. The woman had a reputation for the best oatmeal chocolate chip cookies in town.

As Kit walked to the door, her mind wandered for a moment to the bake sale in support of the animal shelter over a year ago. She and Kat had attended the event in support of the cause — Kit for the food, Kat to get a glimpse of the local veterinarian.

Kat and Evan now had a strong romance, and Kit had chosen to take a back seat in her relationship with Kat so the new lovers could explore their connection together. After her brief encounter with Greg, she had hoped she'd found a partner, too. Her heart urged her to give him another chance, while her head told her to let it go. Or was it the other way around? She released a sigh of frustration at her inability to distinguish between what her heart and head wanted.

Kit brought her attention back to the moment, reached for the door handle, and turned the knob. As soon as she'd pulled the door open, her breath caught in her throat.

Her gaze locked with Greg's baby blues. "Hi," she choked out.

Greg nodded and removed his cowboy hat. She perused

his form from top to bottom, stopping on his hands, rugged and work-worn, and fought a shiver at the thought of those calloused hands caressing her skin. He wore a light blue button-down work shirt, and a pair of blue jeans that fit him to perfection.

She stared, dumbfounded by her reaction to the man. He raised one eyebrow in question, which only made her insides flutter more. Men, in general, did not affect her this way. Due to her job, she kept a professional distance between the men and women she saw as clients. She also needed to have a deep emotional connection with someone to even consider a sexual relationship. But something about Greg melted her insides every time she saw him, and even though she didn't know him well, she felt a connection to him. Never mind that he'd trusted her to bind him with ropes, a gift she cherished.

"Yoo-hoo." Trudy waved a hand in front of her face.

Kit blinked, noticing Trudy for the first time. "Hi," she repeated, then cleared her throat, attempting to return to a more professional demeanour.

"Hey yourself," Trudy said, stepping forward. "Greg agreed to come with me today."

"Indeed," Kit murmured, extending her hand. "Nice to meet you, Greg. Your mother has told me about you."

"I'm sure she has." Greg shook her hand briefly, then dropped it like a hot potato. He brushed by her and walked into the office.

As he passed by, she caught a whiff of his scent—a faint odour of soap and hay. An outdoorsy combination she found oddly intoxicating.

Trudy followed Greg inside, and Kit closed the door behind them, then turned around only to find Greg staring at her, his gaze piercing hers.

With her heart beating a mile a minute, she gestured toward the couch. "Please sit down."

Greg smiled and swept his arm to the side with a slight bow. "Ladies first."

Kit stood straight and walked with professional confidence around the coffee table in the center of the office. Seating herself in the plush chair where she always sat, she opened her notebook and waited for mother and son to seat themselves.

Trudy sat on the couch across from her. Greg plopped down beside his mother and placed his hat in his lap.

"I notice you didn't say she's told you *a lot* about me," Greg stated without preamble.

Kit gestured between mother and son. "Well, according to Trudy, the two of you don't talk much, which would make it difficult to tell me anything about you. And even if she did, I keep everything in confidence."

"Good to know." The corner of his mouth twitched, and the sexy smirk made her stomach quiver.

Kit felt her cheeks heat.

"You two going to get it on, or should we talk?" Trudy interrupted.

Kit composed herself, then wagged a finger at Trudy. "You asked for a session today to tell me all about your date this past weekend. You could have given me a heads up that Greg would be joining us today. I'll have to charge you extra."

Trudy waved a hand. "Girl, I could probably pay you in cookies and you'd still see me."

Kit shrugged. "Maybe, but chocolate chip cookies don't pay the mortgage. And there is such a thing as professional courtesy."

"Touché," Trudy conceded. "I'm sorry I didn't mention it."

"Would you mind explaining why?" Kit asked.

A small snort got Kit's attention. Greg was staring at them with an amused expression on his face. "What?"

"This." Greg waggled a finger between her and Trudy.

"This is great. I haven't met a woman who isn't flustered by my mother's wit."

Kit batted her eyelashes. "I am a professional."

"You think I'm witty, son?" Trudy placed her hand over her heart. "I'll take that as a compliment."

Kit nodded at Trudy. "You are one of a kind."

Trudy narrowed her eyes. "Is *that* a compliment?"

Before Kit could answer, Greg clapped his hands together. "All right. I've got a ranch to get back to, so perhaps we can get this session going. Mom, what is it you wanted to talk to me about and felt better with Kit here?"

Trudy glanced at her wrist. "Well, would you look at the time? I need to get going."

Kit frowned in confusion. "What are you talking about? You just got here, and besides, it's your appointment."

Greg heaved a sigh and folded his arms over his chest. "Mom, you're not even wearing a watch."

Trudy scratched her wrist. "Huh . . . You're right. It must be my intuition telling me it's time to leave." She hiked her purse onto her shoulder and stood. "You kids have a nice chat about me, and we will discuss it next week."

Surprised, Kit gaped as Trudy hurried from the office, slamming the door behind her.

She turned to Greg. "What the hell just happened?"

Greg scratched at his head. "I don't know. She told me she wanted to discuss something with me, but she felt better doing it at your office. Said she felt better with a professional present."

Kit muttered under her breath. "That woman will drive me nuts one day . . ."

One of Greg's eyebrows shot upward. "You're talking about my mother."

Kit rolled her eyes. "As if you don't know your own mother."

"You have a point." He chuckled, lounging back into the sofa, one arm on the backrest, long legs stretched out in front of him. "There were times I thought she'd be the death of me. Or I'd strangle her. But like you said — she is one of a kind."

Kit swallowed hard, trying not to be affected by his sexy sprawl on her couch. Moisture gathered in her pussy, and she pressed her legs together, tugging down her skirt. "Well." She cleared her throat. "Your mom has paid in advance for this session. Tell me how you'd like to proceed on her dime."

"I find it incredibly hot that you don't wear panties," he murmured.

She startled for a second, then zeroed in on him, her Domme persona rising to the challenge. *He needs to be taught a lesson.* Kit straightened her spine, intentionally thrusting out her breasts and crossing one leg over the other slowly to give Greg a good glimpse of what he wouldn't be getting.

She noted Greg's reaction to the red three-inch heels that adorned her feet. She purposefully swung one leg for a second, letting the moment drag out, and relished the way Greg's nostrils flared and his pupils dilated as he observed her actions.

Kit stood, her feet shoulder-width apart, hands on hips, and stared at him. Using her commanding voice, she said, "Correction, slut. The proper response is, I find it incredibly hot that you don't wear panties, *Mistress*."

Greg's cheeks flushed with a pink hue. He sat up straight and bowed his head. "I find it incredibly hot that you don't wear panties, Mistress."

"Better, slut." Kit tapped the toe of one foot against the floor for a moment, then walked around to stand in front of him. She sat on the coffee table and feathered her fingers through his hair. Then she raked her fingernails across his scalp before clutching a handful of hair, tugging his head back hard. Greg's eyes rolled back, and he let out a moan.

Kit sighed and released him, resting her elbows on her knees. "We need to talk, Greg."

He released a heavy sigh. "Yeah, we do."

"Why have you been avoiding me?" Her voice came out small, almost shy — a huge contrast from her more dominant nature. The tone threw her off-guard, and she frowned, wondering where the sudden insecure feelings were coming from. She stood to pace the length of the table, then plopped down into her chair again.

Greg rubbed his palms into his eyes, then stared heavenward for a few moments.

Kit remained silent, waiting for him to speak. Their eyes locked for a moment, and Kit could see a maelstrom of emotions sweep over his expression.

Greg slid off the couch, onto his hands and knees, crawled toward her, then knelt in front of her. "Permission to hold your hands, Mistress?"

Kit nodded, swallowing back the emotion threatening to break free in the form of tears. Her ego tried to whisper that she needed to remain in control, maintain her Domme side to make sure he knew who was in charge. But she did nothing, remaining still, allowing him to express himself. This moment mattered to both of them.

Greg took her hands in his and looked up into her eyes. "I've been avoiding you because I like you."

"I like you, too," she whispered. For several seconds, they stared at each other, unblinking.

Aww . . . We did the same thing. Wait . . . What the fuck? As if cold water had been dumped on her, Kit stood, pushed Greg away, and stomped over to her desk.

"This is impossible." She started pacing across her office. "I'm a therapist. People talk to me about these sorts of things, and I always counsel that honest communication is the best course of action. You and I could not have been avoiding each other for the same reason." She slammed her hands on the top of her desk, then whipped around to face Greg. He'd remained on his knees, watching her. She gestured at him. "Get up."

Greg growled low in his throat, yet loud enough for her to hear. He stood and squared off with her.

Kit pointed a finger at him. "Do not get all uppity with me, mister."

"What are you so angry about?" He threw up his hands in exasperation. "This is why I've been avoiding you. I can't trust you enough to be stable emotionally."

Kit gaped at him, taken aback by his insolence. Then she snapped her mouth shut and gritted her teeth, crossing her arms over her chest. "I am a professional. How dare you accuse me of being emotionally unstable? Do not project your issues with your mother at me."

"And what issues are you projecting at me?" Greg crossed his arms over his chest and narrowed his eyes. "Who is your counsellor, *counsellor*?"

"Well ... I ... well ..." Kit stammered. "I used to see someone regularly, but they moved, and I haven't gotten a referral. I am self-aware. I work on my issues so I don't bring them into any sessions with clients."

"This isn't a session. What we shared wasn't a session. And maybe that's what you have a hard time with." Greg shook his head. "It's always the professionals that think they have all the answers and don't want to work on their own issues. Maybe it was a mistake to come here today."

"Why did you come here?"

Greg sighed again. "Like I said, I figured we needed to talk, especially if we are going into business together." He hung his head for a moment. "It seems we have been avoiding each other for our own reasons, albeit similar ones."

Kit massaged her forehead before speaking. "Okay,

look . . . I didn't know how to handle the situation. You asked me to come over to discuss business plans, then one thing led to another, and you let me tie you up . . ." She sighed. "I really enjoyed it. Your submission was a gift to me."

He raised an eyebrow. "Really? I find that hard to believe. Most people don't accept a gift then leave it behind."

"Well, you didn't exactly give me any feedback," she retorted. "You had an orgasm, so the scene must have been intense for you, but you wouldn't answer any of my questions afterward. I had no idea how to give you any sort of aftercare, and you acted like you didn't need it, never mind want it at all." She growled in frustration and began to pace again. "I mean, with my clients, we discuss all of their needs ahead of time, including what they'd like to happen after a session, but we barely talked when we were finished, and I felt lost, like I had over-stepped."

"It was perfect," he responded. "I was a bit stunned, that's all. When I'm processing emotionally, I have a hard time finding words."

She stopped pacing to stare at him. "You could have said that."

"I wasn't in a space to communicate clearly that night, and I haven't been ready to talk with you yet. Until today that is."

Kit exhaled in exasperation. "You could have said that too. No wonder your mother is worried about you."

"Well, she doesn't have to be." He shrugged. "I'd never felt so at ease with anyone else. Even when I travelled to events, I always felt nervous until I got comfortable in my surroundings. With you, it came easy. No anxiety." He shook his head, appearing confused.

"What?" she asked.

"Well, to be honest, my ego got the better of me."

Kit took a step toward him. "How so?"

Greg scratched his head. "My brain started telling me

things like, *well, of course it was good, it's her job.* Or *she doesn't really care about you, it's what she does for a living. Don't enjoy it — it doesn't mean anything to her . . .* That kind of . . . thing."

"Oh." Kit murmured. "That isn't how I felt at all, Greg." She came to stand in front of him. "To be honest, I haven't had a romantic Domme-sub relationship in quite some time. Kat and I dabbled in BDSM from time to time, but it was a loving exploration. And you're right — I do this for a living. It is why you contacted me to talk business. Which, by the way, is a great idea and something I want to be on board with."

Greg looked down and shuffled his feet. "Thanks. Combining my passions is what I'm focused on." He looked back up. "I know you create a safe space for your clients, and I thought you might want to broaden your horizons a little."

Kit smiled. "I do. I think we'd make great partners. In more ways than one."

"Oh?" Greg's voice held an interested note.

"I'm sorry I avoided you. So many times I scolded myself to break the silence between us, practice what I preach . . . My parents never communicated about anything, and I've consciously chosen to work on it, and help others be better communicators. But when I had someone in my life who mattered . . . I cannot believe I fell into an old pattern." She hung her head, then looked at him again. "I will be more conscious of it, and not let my ego get the better of me." She ran a hand down his arm. "You know the day when you showed up to rescue Evan and Kat from their horse nightmare . . ."

Greg snickered. "Night-*mare* indeed."

Kit giggled. "Yeah, oh, my God, I've never seen a man more inept at dating than Evan."

"And yet they worked it out," Greg commented.

"And I want to work it out between us, too." Kit ran her hand back up his arm.

"Well . . ." Greg raked his fingers through his hair. "I've

never had an ongoing D-s relationship before, and I had no idea how to react. I was embarrassed, I guess, at how I responded to you, and I didn't want you to use it against me."

Shocked, Kit put a hand over her heart. "I would never do such a thing. My professional or personal moral code wouldn't allow me to."

"Yeah, well, I don't know that, do I?" he asked. "I mean, you're my mom's sex therapist, so you obviously have an inkling as to what my issues are with women."

Kit pondered for a moment. "You don't want someone overbearing or controlling in your face. Your mother once mentioned a deal you made with your dad to be a go-between for you and her."

"You got it." He nodded.

"You are a great submissive, Greg. The experience surprised me, too. I felt a connection with you, and I'm unused to that. I don't feel emotional connections with very many people. It's what makes my job easier—providing a service, teaching, helping others learn about their bodies, needs, wants, and desires."

"And what about your needs, wants, and desires?" His words came out low when he spoke.

The deep tone of his voice sent a shudder through her insides. "I . . . I get pleasure from helping people. I don't often think about what I need."

Greg reached out and played with a strand of her hair. "Pity. I would pleasure you in any way you demanded."

For the first time in a long time, Kit blushed at a man's compliment. "Thank you. I'd never take advantage of that."

Greg chuckled. "I know, or at least I think I do. You would be worth worshipping." He sighed. "I like being in control of my life, but I enjoy giving up that control in controlled situations. You were . . . *are* the best I've ever had." He shook his head. "When I saw you joking around with Marty, my ego took another swing at me. I got jealous thinking of how many men you *help*."

Kit chuckled, then clapped a hand over her mouth. "Without breaking confidentiality, it's the women I help most in this town. Men are too intimidated by me."

Greg grinned from ear to ear. "Well, my ego will take that one for a win."

Kit framed his face in her hands. "Would you like to discuss the terms of a relationship with me?"

Greg glanced around her office, then stared back into her eyes. "I believe I would."

Kit stepped back from him, then took his hand. "Then follow me."

Greg grasped her hand as she led him to the door at the back of the room. When she opened it, it was like stepping down into another world. While her office was a cheery light colour, her dungeon room was a warm contrast.

As he descended the stairs, Greg let out a low whistle and looked around. Kit followed his gaze, trying to see it through his eyes. The space was decorated in several dark wood colours. It gave the room a cozy feel, yet spoke of a person's deepest, most sensual desires. Various wooden apparatuses were pressed up against the length of one wall—a St. Andrew's cross, spanking horse, kneeling bench, and several chairs with different attachments for cuffing or tying people into different positions.

Two wooden chests and an armoire were in the opposite corner. A day bed was pushed against another wall, the rich, satiny hues of the multi-coloured pillows and throw blankets offered an inviting place to play or to rest after a session. A plush rocking chair and some over-sized bean bag chairs were up against another wall. The center of the room was empty, waiting for the next client's desire to fill it.

"This is a wonderful space." Greg's voice was filled with

awe. "Better than any dungeon I've ever been in."

Kit nodded. "Thank you. There are a few seamstresses here in town that I ask to make pillows and blankets on occasion just to change things up a bit." She pointed at the chests. "One contains toys, the other blankets and pillows in case a client has a favourite that I don't have laid out already. I like people to have their comforts."

"I'm sure you think of everything." Greg gestured toward the armoire. "May I?"

"You have permission."

Kit followed as Greg walked to the armoire. Once there, he opened the doors and gasped in surprise. Lengths of rope in every colour imaginable hung on the inside, along with paddles, wooden spoons, canes, cuffs, leashes, and more. Everything had a place, all in order, so a client could choose what they wanted with ease.

Greg turned to her with an expression of sincerity. "I definitely need you to organize this sort of thing for me. There's everything anyone could want in here, not to mention it's colourful and inviting. Exactly the kind of thing I want to create."

Kit nodded. "I like tidiness and order. Makes a good experience for everyone." She cocked her head and fingered a length of pink rope. "I also like people to be able to play with colours, not just sensations. The keyword for me is and always has been *play*. People should feel free to explore and play with their sexuality."

"Huh." Greg paused for a moment. "That seems like a really healthy way to look at it."

"It's the way I see it."

Greg walked around the room, touching all the apparatuses, taking in the erotic art on the walls. He sat on the edge of the end of the bed, fingers brushing over the satiny sheets and fuzzy fleece blankets. "You've thought of everything. This is amazing."

"Well, I try to anticipate people's needs. If I don't have something, then I find a way to get it so they can have it the next time. I would like to have more toys." She pointed to the other chest. "I have lots of dildos and plugs, but some fucking machines or a Sybian would be nice. Lots of women would love to try those."

Greg covered his ears. "Please don't tell me my mother is a client."

Kit laughed. "Your mother has never seen the inside of this room."

"Thank God," he muttered.

"I do, however, have a lot of insight into her sex life. Not that I can divulge anything to you," she said. "Client-therapist confidentiality and all that."

"Thank God my mom doesn't have any idea about what I'm into."

Kit took hold of his hand. "You underestimate her. I wouldn't put it past her to have some insight—you are her son, after all. She probably knows you better than you think. She did trick you into coming here."

Greg humphed. "I thought she had something important to share with me and wanted support. She duped both of us." He shook his head. "I can't believe she thinks I could benefit from sex therapy. I know myself better than she thinks."

"Your mom is learning about herself, and sometimes when people gain insights into themselves, they often feel they need their loved ones to experience something similar." Kit smiled. "It happens all the time."

Greg narrowed his eyes. "You aren't angry that she tricked you?"

Kit pondered a moment. "A little annoyed. But I will deal with that the next time I see her. Not sure I will thank her, even though she did bring us together."

"Yeah, I am not giving that woman one iota of credit." Greg grimaced. "I'd never hear the end of it."

"Tell me about that." Kit sat on the edge of the bed beside him and crossed her legs.

Greg wrapped her in a tight hug, rubbing his chin into the crook of her neck. "I don't need a counsellor, counsellor."

Kit squealed and squirmed out of his embrace. She hadn't realized she'd gone into counsel mode. "I'm sorry. When I feel someone has an issue, I want to help." She held her hands up to halt his protests. "I don't want you to feel like I want to fix you. I want to get to know you better."

"Can't you let me reveal things in my own time?"

"But will you? And are you saying I'm not allowed to ask questions?"

Greg's blank expression didn't give her anything to work with. She opened her mouth to apologize, then snapped it closed. She would not apologize for being her. If he wouldn't give her the benefit of the doubt as to her good intentions, then she wouldn't waste time trying to convince him.

Annoyance rose within her, and she did nothing to stop it. Greg's stubbornness to communicate only on his terms would drive her crazy in the long run. She'd promised herself that any relationship she'd enter would be based on open communication as the foundation for intimacy. How did she do that with someone who refused to share himself unless he wanted to?

Kit stood and smoothed down her skirt. She looked Greg straight in the eye and gestured at the door that led upstairs. "Please show yourself out." Then she turned and walked over to one of the armoires and made a show of organizing the contents. She waited to hear the door closing, but no sound came. After a few moments, she dared to turn around.

Greg was still sitting on the bed, staring at her. "I refuse to be dismissed." The grumbly tone of his voice carried a hint of dejection.

"And I refuse to pull your teeth to get you to talk. I'm not into torture as pleasure." She gestured between them. "This will never work."

"It will never work if you want to be my therapist," he countered. "I don't want one, nor do I feel I need one."

She released an exasperated sigh. "Then what do you want? Because if I can't ask questions to get to know you, without you accusing me of trying to fix you, then this will never work, and you know it. It's like you're trying to sabotage us before we begin."

"And what about you? You were quick to pass judgment that this wouldn't work," he said.

Anger rose within her once more, and she wanted to protest. Instead, she let it go. Greg had a point. Her parents' inability to communicate had been the reason she'd become a therapist. She'd switched to sex therapy when she realized that sexual intimacy had been the one area of their lives where people most often had trouble communicating.

"You're right. I chose sex therapy as a way to work through my issues with my parents. I wanted to be as healthy as I could be for any of my relationships. What I've realized over the years by helping others and doing my own work is that relationships trigger us to see deeper into our issues in order to resolve them. Our relationship is no different." Kit walked back over and sat down beside him. "Greg, I don't feel you need fixing. What I want is to create a healthy partnership with you. The only way I know how to do that is to talk to you, ask you questions about yourself. I'm being as honest with you as I can. Are you willing to do the same for me?"

Greg's Adam's apple bobbed when he swallowed, but he didn't respond. He looked a like a deer caught in the headlights. Kit massaged her brow for a moment and decided to keep talking. Maybe if she opened up to him more, he would feel comfortable to share with her. And if she didn't express what she wanted, and needed, she would only have herself to blame when her needs weren't met.

"I want to be in a relationship with someone who will talk to me about anything and everything. Sex might be important, but at the end of the day, if I can't talk to someone about my childhood, my issues, or how my day went, or just be silly with them . . ." She blew a breath upward. "Then it's not the relationship for me." She ran her fingertips down his forearm. "No matter how much I might like someone."

Greg heaved a sigh. "Talking has never been my specialty." He took her hands in his. "I stopped talking to my mom the first time I heard her gossiping about something to a friend. I worried that whatever I told her would be blabbed to anyone who would listen." He looked heavenward. "I love my mother dearly, but she cannot keep a secret to save her life. I know it's who she is, but I didn't want my life, and all the things I do in a day, to be public knowledge."

Kit rubbed his shoulder. "I get that, I really do. For me, it was the opposite."

"What do you mean?" He turned toward her more, brushing back some hair behind her ear.

She gave him a half smile. "My parents didn't talk to me about much. They didn't even speak to each other. Every conversation was awkward, especially about sex. I grew up determined I would be comfortable with who I was and talk to people about anything and everything."

He nodded. "Okay . . . fair enough."

She shrugged a shoulder and winked at him. "Self-responsibility is my game. Although I admit, even now my issues get the better of me, and I have to work on it."

He chuckled, then sighed again. "I am aware I have transferred my issues with my mom to women in general. I realize not all women are gossiping hens, but I treat them all like they are. I don't trust anyone easily . . . if at all."

She squeezed his hands. "I promise that anything you ever say to me will never be uttered to a single soul unless you tell me it's okay." She placed a hand over her heart. "I would never betray anyone that way, especially someone I care about."

He traced her jaw with a fingertip. "I believe you. But I need you to be patient with me as I transition to fully trusting you."

"Does this mean you want more than a business arrangement?" Even she heard the hopeful note in her voice. She held her breath, waiting for his answer.

Greg stared into her eyes for several heartbeats. Then he got onto his knees in front of her and placed his hands behind his back. "Kit Morgan, would you be my Domme?"

CHAPTER THREE

Greg's heart pounded in his chest while he waited with bated breath for Kit to answer. He'd never played with a Domme before—in fact, he'd never been in a serious relationship with a woman, either. Sure, he'd had sex with women, mostly one-night stands, but his experiences as a sub had never been sexual. He'd found Doms at conventions he'd attended, conversed with them about his needs, then been tied up, flogged, or spanked. He'd trusted those men to deliver what he needed with no attachments or emotional intimacy. It had been a contract plain and simple. With Kit, there was potential for so much more. And he wanted it as much as it fucking scared the shit out of him.

Nervous energy coursed through his system as seconds ticked by. When he thought he'd burst from anticipation, he noticed tears forming in her eyes, and she nodded her head.

Her whispered words were magic to his ears. "Yes, I'd love to be your Domme."

Greg grinned from ear to ear, then bowed his head. "Thank you, Mistress."

Kit took his face in her hands and made him look at her again. "But wait. There is a lot to discuss. This is a big deal for both of us. I mean, I'm bisexual. And being with women is a part of myself I don't want to give up."

Greg frowned. "So, you want an open relationship?" He sat back on his haunches, considering.

Kit cocked her head to the side. "I feel what would work best for me is for us to have a primary relationship."

"What does that mean to you?" Greg asked.

"From time to time," she began, "I'd like to bring a woman home to play with. Kat was one of my regular play partners until she and Evan entered a relationship. Even though we've had a couple of threesomes, they've told me they want to focus on each other right now."

"Huh . . . Okay." He licked his lips, conjuring up the image in his mind of Kit and his friends sharing sexual playtime. "I admit I find it hot that you all have played together. I am a voyeur at heart."

Kit raised an eyebrow. "Would you like to watch us play some time?"

Greg rubbed the stubble on his chin. "I believe I would, although it's not something I've truly considered as an option before. As long as Evan and Kat would be up for it."

Kit smiled. "Well, he's a pretty open-minded guy for someone so seemingly reserved. He's willing to experiment and learn. I'm happy Kat found someone who encourages her and is willing to explore their sexuality together. At any rate, we could talk about it with them and see how they feel. Communication is key with potential play partners."

Greg ducked his head, cheeks heating at the thought of what he was about to admit out loud. "I would like to have that kind of partnership with you." He cleared his throat, then looked her in the eye again. "I'm all right with you playing with other women from time to time, if it's what you need. I ask that if you wish to play with a man, please communicate with me about it first."

"Absolutely," she agreed.

"And you know, maybe, we could ask Evan and Kat about how they feel about me watching some time."

Kit beamed. "This excites me."

"Me too. Kind of makes me nervous, though."

Kit cupped his jaw. "I totally understand. It's not something we have to rush into. I would like to establish our relationship first before we truly act on these scenarios."

Greg's heart was beating a mile a minute. Getting over

himself wouldn't be an easy task, yet if the current conversation was any indication, he and Kit were off to a good start. He'd told himself all sorts of tall tales over the years to mask his insecurities—how a woman would find him weak for being submissive, that they would never understand, that it would be too difficult to find someone to communicate with.

In truth, he'd led a loner life on purpose to avoid any possibility of rejection. Sure, he'd felt accepted when he'd gone to conventions—then again, that had been the point. People attended those events to meet other kinksters, which he enjoyed, but he kept everyone at arm's length. Even though he stayed in touch with some of them through email or social media, he'd always been glad to come home and maintain a distance, because it meant he didn't have to be emotionally invested or accountable twenty-four-seven.

The woman before him, offering herself to him as his Domme, had shattered his illusions in a matter of minutes. He could no longer tell himself any of the old stories anymore. Kit sat there open and willing to talk about anything and everything important to him. So much for keeping to himself. Thank goodness he finally felt ready to take the leap into a real relationship.

"I'm a little scared," he blurted.

Kit blinked in surprise but spoke in a warm tone that put him at ease. "Scared of what, hon?"

Her gaze scanned his face as if searching for some clue to his distress, and it caused his heart to pound harder. He wanted to kiss her senseless, as much to convince himself she was real, as to show her how much he wanted what she offered.

Greg swallowed hard. "This. Us." He gestured between them. "I've told myself, over and over, that I'd never find a woman who would understand my submissive needs, never mind all the stories I've told myself about how women can't be trusted . . ." He continued to stare at her and cleared his throat. "There's something you should know."

Her eyebrows scrunched together. "What is it?"

"You're the first Domme I've ever had."

Kit embraced him, burying her head in the crook of his neck. "I'm not surprised."

"You're not?"

She shook her head. "You keep to yourself and are particular about who you interact with. My guess is that you've chosen Doms to fulfill needs on occasions that were not sexual in nature."

Greg blinked in surprise. "Wow. You're good."

Kit leaned back from him and shrugged a shoulder. "A hunch. It doesn't surprise me that you chose to explore your sexuality in a manner that felt safe to you."

Greg scratched at his head. "Yeah, I did. I didn't have to worry about them hitting on me or asking me for something I couldn't give."

"Kind of like the kink version of going for a beer with the guys?" She accompanied her statement with a wink.

He grinned, then chuckled. "Yeah, I suppose. No commitment, just camaraderie."

Kit cupped his cheek in her hand, then placed a gentle kiss on his lips. "I cherish your honesty and your personal integrity to do what feels right for you. I expect you to do the same in our relationship. This isn't about me telling you what to do the whole time. I want you to choose what you want, the language that feels best for you. If I say or do something that doesn't feel right to you, I expect you to communicate with me. Deal?"

"Deal." Greg threaded his hands into her hair, savouring the warmth left from her lips. In that moment, he threw caution to the wind and initiated a kiss, thrusting his tongue inside her mouth, losing himself to her taste.

Kit reciprocated, and their kiss became one long, drawn-out moment of desire. Greg focused on himself, diving down to a place inside he rarely let himself go. His body buzzed in excitement as he allowed the passion to echo through his system. Their tongues twined in a lazy fashion. His cock swelled, his balls ached, and he longed to feel her hand smacking his ass, the sting of pain made sweeter by the woman delivering the blow.

Kit pulled back a bit, then bit his lip . . . hard. He gasped as the pain sent a surge of pleasure through his body. He stared into her face, vision blurred from passion, breath heaving, waiting for her instruction.

Kit surprised him with a heavy-handed slap to his face, the shock of it sending a jolt through his body along with a thrill. He gasped, but not in pain. The slap wasn't one of anger, nor was it meant to humiliate. The delivery had been for the shock value, to garner his attention. Her hand remained on his face, the warmth from her palm permeating his skin.

She leaned forward and whispered into his ear, her husky tone and warm breath sent a shiver down his spine. "You need to ask Mistress for permission to kiss her."

Greg swayed as dizziness washed over him, a heady experience to be dominated by someone he cared about and who cared for him. "Yes, Mistress." He licked his lips, collecting his wits to ask an important question. "Is this something you want me to do on a regular basis?"

Kit smiled. "Yes. I think that when either of one of us wants a need fulfilled, or we are feeling sexual and want to act on it, we ask for permission. I will also do the same for you, and not assume that you are at my beck and call all the time. Does that work for you, slut?"

He nodded, eager to continue. "Yes, Mistress."

She ducked her head to look into his eyes. "Mistress was

pleased with that kiss and cannot wait to see how skilled you are in other areas." She wiggled her eyebrows.

Heart pounding a happy rhythm, he grinned like a fool. "I am eager to please you in any way you desire, Mistress."

Kit took hold of his chin and gave him a loving squeeze. "Good. But now I want to get to know you better." She released him and stood. "What would you like most right now?"

Elated, Greg stammered his reply. "I, uh, um . . . Well, I want to be spanked by you again."

She raised an eyebrow. "Oh?"

He inhaled a deep breath to calm himself. "I want you to spank me, Mistress."

She nodded in approval. "Better."

Greg bowed his head. "Please, Mistress, please spank me."

"Ah, even better." She placed her index finger under his chin and lifted it, indicating for him to look at her. "Come with me."

Kit turned on her heels, and he followed her to a padded bench. He helped her pull it away from the wall, then stood motionless, hands behind his back, awaiting further instruction.

He watched with eagerness as Kit opened an armoire and fingered a few implements, finally choosing a flogger and a paddle, then she turned back to him. "Remove your pants and underwear." She pressed a fingertip to her lips, studying him. "On second thought . . . take off all your clothing."

He did as she commanded and stood naked, ass cheeks clenching in anticipation.

"Bend over the bench," she instructed. "Place your chin on the pad at the top, legs braced on the floor, arms hanging down."

Greg complied, and for a moment he felt vulnerable with his ass on display, the cool air on his heated skin reminding him that he had given up control. But when Kit ran the paddle over both his ass cheeks, he sighed in contentment and surrendered to the moment.

Kit walked to the front of the bench and bent forward to look him in the eyes. He appreciated that she'd chosen to communicate this way to avoid misunderstandings.

"I want to cuff your wrists and ankles to the hooks on the sides here." She indicated the metal welded to the legs.

"Yes, Mistress."

"Good." She gave a pert nod. "And while I have your attention, no coming until I tell you to. Is that understood?"

"Yes, Mistress."

Out of the corner of his eye, Greg watched Kit retrieve two sets of cuffs from the armoire. With gentle care, she cuffed each wrist and ankle to the bench. He wriggled for good measure, thrilled when he couldn't move. It scared him a little to advance their relationship this way—trusting her to give him the release he needed and be vulnerable to her at the same time. He reminded himself that he'd already done this once with her, and they had communicated far more today than they had previously. His panic was nothing other than his old worries trying to reassert themselves in his consciousness, and they had no place there.

"Breathe," Kit encouraged.

Greg closed his eyes, inhaled deeply through his nostrils, and let out a slow breath from his mouth. He continued the breathing pattern, concentrating on sensation. Kit started with a few hard smacks with her bare hands. His cock grew hard, and he willed himself not to come.

Greg wriggled a bit when she stopped the spanking, wondering what she had planned next. He bit his lip to suppress a groan when the strands of the flogger trailed over his ass and backs of his legs. His body tensed in excitement.

"Relax," Kit soothed.

He tried, but the moment she brought the flogger down onto his bare flesh, he flinched, followed by a shiver. He couldn't help it. He loved the sting, especially amplified after she'd already spanked him with her bare hands. It upped the ante for him, brought him to heightened awareness. With each whack on his flesh, he released a breath, and his body eventually relaxed as he grew accustomed to the bite on his skin.

Kit flogged his ass, hamstrings, and calves, alternating with light strokes on his back and hips. He loved the varying sensations, craved the light strokes mixed with the heavy-handed ones. Limp in his restraints, he took what she gave, his cock and balls swollen with need.

Kit stopped her ministrations, and he waited, attempting to catch his breath. She came around to the front again and knelt within his vision. She brushed her fingertips over his cheeks and looked into his eyes. "How are you doing, slut?"

Greg wet his lips and trembled at her use of the word *slut*. He'd longed to embrace his slutty side with someone he trusted. "Good, Mistress."

"Do you want more?" she asked.

"Yes, please, Mistress."

She placed the flogger down on the floor in front of him and showed him the paddle. "I want to use this on you now. Do you feel you could take it?"

Greg tried to nod, but his restrained position made it difficult. "Yes, Mistress."

"Okay." She feathered her fingers through his hair. "This is the wrong time to ask, but do you have a safe word? I apologize for not asking earlier."

The tenderness in her gaze touched his heart. "I've always used the word *salt*," he whispered.

"Salt it is."

She placed a gentle kiss to his forehead, stood, and walked

around to the rear of the bench once more. Greg felt the flat of the paddle smooth over his ass cheeks as if she were spreading butter on toast. The cool surface of the paddle felt good on his heated skin.

Kit commanded that he count this time, so he called out the number with each swat she delivered. The first stung, and he moaned out loud. She delivered blows to each ass cheek, getting harder with each one. His body shuddered, but he kept count.

When he reached the count of ten, he was breathing hard and had entered a euphoric state, one he hadn't encountered before. Coherent thought left his brain. His whole body felt alive and electric. Kit reminded him to use his safe word, but he declined, barely remembering to address her correctly.

She instructed him to thank her after each smack. His breathless words of *Thank you, Mistress* became a rhythm unto themselves. When the next set of ten ended, delirium had set in. He'd never experienced this kind of euphoria before. Emotion overwhelmed him, and he didn't know what to do. Vulnerability swamped him, and he opened his mouth to use his safe word.

Before he could speak, Kit ran her hands over his ass cheeks with such loving tenderness, it brought tears to his eyes. Greg began to sob, body shaking in the restraints.

He couldn't speak, and his brain tried to tell him to stop embarrassing himself, or Kit would think him a fool. He did not register her unlocking the cuffs until she grabbed hold of his arm and helped lift his torso off the bench. His wobbly legs wouldn't support him, and he collapsed in a heap. Kit followed him down, and it surprised him when his ass hit softness. He hadn't noticed that she'd placed pillows and blankets on the floor.

Greg wanted to apologize, ask her to forgive his weakness, and tell her it wouldn't happen next time. But as Kit cradled his head to her chest, whispering words of reassurance and wrapping a blanket around them both, he couldn't find any words to express what he truly felt at that moment.

Instead, he snuggled into her loving embrace and let the tears flow, feeling safe for the first time in his life. "Thank you, Mistress," he whispered between sobs.

"You're welcome," she said in a hushed tone.

Greg concentrated on her—her arms around him, her scent, her breasts cushioning his head. Processing through his tears, he allowed himself to feel loved.

CHAPTER FOUR

"You're an excellent rigger," Kit praised.

"Thank you." Greg tugged on the rope in his hand, hoisting her up off the ground.

Kit let out a squeal as she hung suspended, the cool air pebbling her naked flesh. Time seemed to have flown by in the past few weeks since they'd put a lot of their time and effort into renovations out at his farm.

Currently, they were in the midst of a break from stocking the dressers and armoires in the barn with sex toys.

Greg had tied her upper body in a beautiful harness of elegant knots that went around her breasts, accentuating her taut nipples. Her body remained upright, with her arms tied behind her back. Her left leg was positioned straight out to the side with a rope tied to an ankle cuff, then connected to the rigging above her. Her right leg was tied bent at the knee with her ankle secured to the back of her thigh. Once he'd finished that, he attached ropes hanging from the ceiling and lifted her further into the air on the suspension rigging.

He grinned, tugging on a couple of the knots, testing his handiwork. "I've always been fascinated by ropes, rope play, being suspended. I figured the best way to learn why I liked rope play was to learn how to do it as well as have it done to me." He stepped back to inspect the scene. "Damn, woman, you're flexible. You comfortable?"

Kit waggled her eyebrows. "Very comfortable. And I work on keeping in shape. Flexibility always comes in handy during sex."

"Indeed, it does."

His voice came out in a low growl, making Kit shiver, or rather, her body tried to in its immobilized state. Greg had done an excellent job. Always playing the part of Domme, she'd never been in this vulnerable of a position with anyone before. Uncharacteristic emotions overwhelmed her.

Greg cocked his head with an inquisitive stare. "Are you okay? I can bring you down," he offered. "I wanted to show you what I could do to see if you thought I would be able to run a workshop."

She swallowed the lump in her throat, her voice sounding hoarse even to her own ears. "I think you'd do a great job. The way you explained everything you were doing while you tied me, you'd be brilliant at this."

"Then what's wrong?" He brushed his fingers down the side of her cheek. "You can trust me."

"I know," she whispered. "And that's just it . . . I finally found someone I can trust this way."

"Aww . . ." He looked at her with such tenderness that she feared an all-out crying jag.

"Stop looking at me like that." She sniffed back tears and tried to shake away the emotion.

"Stop looking at you like what?" Greg tapped her nose with a fingertip. "I'm afraid I cannot stop staring at you like a beautiful goddess I am privileged to worship daily."

Kit rolled her eyes at his compliment. "Oh, please . . ."

Greg tweaked each of her nipples. "Oh, please what?"

She gasped at the sensation, and her Domme persona rose to the surface. "I didn't give you permission to touch me that way, slut."

His eyes narrowed, and a feral expression spread across his face. "Are you going to punish me, Mistress?"

Kit relaxed, thankful in the moment for the distraction Greg had provided. She ignored his obvious request for punishment and began to talk business. "I want to hold a workshop for you to teach this as soon as possible. Begin with the basics, then keep adding workshops once people learn the fundamental skill. We can always keep running basic workshops for beginners, which will draw in new people."

"Sounds good," he agreed. "Now to convince people to travel to buttfuck middle of nowhere to partake."

"Hey," she admonished. "Do not put yourself down. You have worked hard on this project, made all sort of contacts all over the world. Besides, together, we will make this work."

A lopsided smile quirked one corner of his mouth. "Yeah, you're right. We make a good team. With your added expertise, we will be able to do a hell of a lot. More than I could on my own."

"Yes, exactly." Tears welled up in her eyes again, the pure joy in her heart radiating throughout her body.

"Are you okay?" he asked again. "You seem . . . more emotional than usual. Not that there is anything wrong with that," he added quickly. "I just . . . well, I want you to be able to be vulnerable with me too. We've played a lot the past few weeks in between work, and while I appreciate the safe spaces you've created for me to explore, I want to be sure I do the same for you."

Kit shook her head and relaxed in the rigging. "I'm happy," she admitted. "Really happy, and tears seem to be the response of the day." A stray tear rolled down one cheek.

He wiped the liquid away with a fingertip. "Do you want to get down?"

"No."

"All right, then."

Kit considered for a moment. He'd done such a great job of tying her that she didn't have to struggle to remain in position. Her pussy clenched as the cool air hit her heated skin and the moisture gathering there. She understood why subs enjoyed this so much. It was freeing to be helpless and used as a fucktoy. But she'd bet her sweet ass she could still top Greg even from this position.

"May I say something?" he asked.

"Of course." She nodded.

He cleared his throat. "These past few weeks have been amazing. I . . . I know I've shied away from sex since our last session, but I have appreciated all the communication and being able to work with you on the dungeons and the main event room, not to mention implementing all of your marketing ideas." He paused, then let out a sigh. "We're going to do it, aren't we?"

"Yes, we are." She never meant three words more in her life.

Understanding dawned in his eyes. "Oh, you're happy too, eh?"

She grinned from ear to ear. "Yes, I am, Greg. I didn't think I had any dreams left until you came along. Then you showed me there were more and helped me make all of them come true."

Greg knelt in front of her. "Well, what can I do for you, Mistress?"

Her heart thumped in her chest. "Take off those pants and show me your cock, slut."

His nostrils flared at her command. "With pleasure." He stood, unzipped his jeans, and slid them down his legs. She noted he'd gone al fresco, and his swollen cock jutted out in her direction. The cock rings he wore gave her a thrill.

Kit let out a slow breath. "I love that you wear your cock rings without being told, my pet."

"I'm glad you approve, Mistress."

His hands twitched at his sides, and she knew how much he wanted to stroke his cock until it grew harder. "Good slut, not touching your cock until Mistress tells you to."

"Thank you, Mistress."

"Now, get on your knees and eat my cunt."

"Yes, Mistress." He dropped to his knees in front of her. He cupped her ass cheeks in his hands and brought her pussy to his lips.

He tasted with tentative licks, and Kit moaned her delight. As a professional Domme, she took satisfaction in giving others what they needed. With Greg, she relished dominating him and receiving pleasure from him at her command.

Greg took his time, flicking his tongue over her clit. She demanded he fingerfuck her pussy and lick her ass. With an eagerness that warmed her heart, he did as she commanded.

Kit continued to give him instructions, and he complied with each of her requests. She closed her eyes, losing herself to sensations as his warm, wet tongue flicked over her clit and his fingers pumped in and out of her cunt.

"Faster," she commanded. His tongue flicked faster over her clit. With each stroke of his fingers, he hit her G-spot, bringing her closer to the edge of orgasm. "Suck my clit hard," she demanded. When he did, waves of pleasure washed through her body as her orgasm exploded.

"Oh fuck," she cried out, then opened her eyes. "Fuck me, slut. Ram your hard cock into my cunt, but no coming."

"Yes, Mistress." Greg stood, and adjusted the rigging, lifting her up a little higher. Then he positioned himself in front of her, his cockhead poised against her opening. He cupped her ass cheeks in his hands once more and waited.

"Good slut, for waiting." She smiled, feeling his cock pulse against her pussy. She waited another few heartbeats before commanding, "Now."

Greg thrust into her, and she cried out. At first, his thrusts were slow, establishing a rhythm. At her urging, he plunged his cock into her with increasing speed. Another orgasm built until she yelled out her release.

Kit could feel Greg's body shudder as her cunt clenched around his cock. As instructed, he was holding back his own release, and she wanted to make him wait a little longer. She allowed him to fuck her until she reached another orgasm, then she demanded to be released from the rigging.

Greg quickly obeyed, gently lowering her to the ground and laying her on her side. Then with adept swiftness, he unknotted his handiwork. When she was freed, he stepped away, hands behind his back and head bowed, to await further instruction.

For a few moments, she lay still on the floor, staring at his swollen cock bobbing up and down, the black cock rings secure at the base. By the look on his face, she could tell he was holding himself in check, but it bordered on torture.

She held out a hand, and he helped her to stand. Her legs wobbled, and with tender care, he placed his arms around her to steady her. Even in his aroused state, he attended to her with such love.

Her hand found his cock, and she stroked. A breath hissed from his mouth, but he remained in control, one of the things she loved most about him as a sub. His need to be used matched her need to dominate.

She slipped one of the cock rings off, and he gritted his teeth, a small groan emanating from the back of his throat. She stroked him again, his cock slick with her juices. "Mmmm . . . You made Mistress so wet when you fucked her and made her come. I am pleased."

When he answered, his voice was low and gravelly. "Thank you, Mistress."

She got on her knees between his legs. "As a reward, I want to clean your cock. But no coming."

"Yes, Mistress." Greg braced his legs further apart, hands clasped behind his back.

Kit enveloped the length of his cock with her mouth, sucking as she pulled back slowly, enjoying her taste on him. She took her time licking him clean while intermittently stroking him. He grew harder, but to his credit, he didn't come.

Kit released his cock from her grip and gave him one last lick. Then she stood, walked over to one of the dressers, opened the drawer, and took out a small, black anal dildo. She popped open a tube of lube and smeared some on the toy, all while keeping an eye on Greg.

Greg's eyes widened, but he said nothing. Kit held the dildo in front of her and walked over to stand in front of him. "I'm going to put this in your ass, slut."

"Yes, Mistress."

"Bend over and brace yourself on the dresser," she instructed.

Kit used the dildo to tease Greg's asshole while reaching between his legs to stroke his cock and balls. She took her time in working the toy into his ass, taking care to go slow and make sure his hole relaxed. When the dildo had been pushed all the way in, Greg let out a long moan.

Kit stroked his cock in earnest, tapping the end of the dildo in rhythm with her strokes. Guttural grunts emanated from Greg, and he involuntarily began to thrust with her actions.

"Uh-uh," she admonished. "Remain still."

Greg gripped the top of the dresser, knuckles whitening as he hung on.

Kit decided it was time to reward him. She leaned forward and whispered into his ear. "Come for me, slut."

Greg groaned, his body shuddering. Kit stroked faster, squeezing his cock a little harder. His body shook with his release, his cum spurting out. Kit continued to stroke, catching some of his cum and smearing it down his length.

Kit licked the shell of his ear. "How was that, slut? Worth the wait?"

"Fuck, yes," Greg murmured.

Kit pulled the dildo out of his ass in one swift movement. "Fuck yes what, slut?"

Greg shouted out as his body shuddered with another orgasm. "Fuck yes, Mistress."

"Good slut." She swatted him hard on each ass cheek.

Greg groaned again, remaining braced against the dresser.

Kit loved the way he always waited for instructions. Satiated, she ran her fingers through his hair. "How about we get something to eat, then we can decide if we want to play some more, or finish painting that one wall?"

Greg chuckled, then turned his head to look at her. "Does this mean I can stand up now, Mistress?"

Kit giggled. "Yes, you can, if your legs will hold you, Greg."

Greg let out a moan, stretched his arms over his head. Then to her surprise, he scooped her up in his arms. "Did that please you, Mistress?"

She looped her arms around his neck. "Yes, it did. But I thought we agreed that you don't have to call me Mistress all the time."

He kissed her nose. "Yeah, but I like to."

She pressed her lips to his. "All right. I can't say as I mind."

"Where to?" he asked.

"Kitchen?"

He grunted. "That's a long walk to carry you—"

She slapped at his arm. "Don't even say it." She squirmed in his embrace, trying to get down.

"Just teasing," he said. "I'm racking up punishment points." He winked.

"Well, in that case, I better keep tally." She chuckled.

The sound of a voice calling out made him pause in his stride. "Oh, my God," he said.

Kit slid down from his arms. "Your mother has impeccable timing."

He didn't hide the annoyance in his voice. "I told her I was busy today."

"At least I don't have you tied up right now," she said. "I better find a robe or something."

Greg snorted. "Yeah . . ." He eyed their naked forms. "We can't exactly greet her like this."

Kit shrugged a shoulder. "Maybe we should. That'll teach her to call first."

Greg laughed. "I love you, Kit."

Kit blushed, happiness invading her heart. "I love you, what?"

Greg's eyes held a feral glint. "I love you, Mistress."

"Damn right you do, slut." She winked at him, then framed his face in her hands. She opened her mouth to return the sentiment, but the sound of Trudy's voice calling out again interrupted her confession.

Greg grimaced. It figured, the minute he confessed his love to the woman of his dreams, his mother had to interrupt the moment. Why couldn't he have waited until he knew they wouldn't be disturbed? He had the worst timing for stuff like this.

He watched Kit rummage in one of the armoires for a robe. Why hadn't she said it back? What if she didn't love him? Did it matter? They were building a life together, both personally and professionally. For the moment, he assured himself that, in time, she would reciprocate the feelings. Even so, his ego tried to whisper otherwise, and he did his best to ignore it.

"Yoo-hoo . . ." Trudy's sing-song voice reached his ears again.

Annoyed, he decided he needed to take charge of this situation. "Wait here," he told Kit, then grabbed a straw cowboy hat that hung on the wall as decoration and held it in front of his cock.

Greg grinned at Kit, winked, then opened the door to greet

his mother. He shut the door behind him, stood in a wide stance, cowboy hat over his erection, and cleared his throat. "Hello, mother."

Trudy had been admiring the space, and his sudden presence obviously startled her. She yelped, then bent over and put a hand over her heart. "Jesus, Mary, and Joseph . . . You gave me a fright. Trying to give your mother a heart attack?" She straightened, and her mouth dropped open when she spotted him, her eyes bugging out in apparent shock. "What in the hell are you doing?"

Greg gestured with his free hand. "If you had called first, you would have known I was busy. This is my way of asking you not to come over unannounced."

"What in hell's half-acre are you doing out here half . . . er, naked?" she asked.

"That's not your business." Greg rocked back on his heels and stared her straight in the eye.

Trudy gaped at him, attempting to stutter a reply. Finally, she said, "I . . . I can't talk to you when you're in that state."

"Then perhaps you could come back another time when I'm not busy."

His mother frowned. "What is going on?"

"When I'm ready to tell you, I will."

Trudy placed her hands on her hips and huffed. "Fine." She turned on her heels, but the sound of a car on the gravel drive caused them both to crane their necks.

Oh, crap. He'd forgotten that Evan and Kat were stopping by to see the dungeons to give them feedback before they opened for business.

Trudy regarded him with a shrewd expression. "Why didn't you say you were having company? I would have understood. You didn't have to come out dressed like that to scare me away." Her lower lip stuck out in a pout.

Greg coughed to suppress his laughter at the look on his

mother's face — that of a child who had a favourite toy taken away. "I told you I was busy today. Why wasn't that enough of an answer without me going into detail?"

Greg heard the door open behind him and turned his head as Kit came to stand beside him. She'd put on one of the robes they had placed in armoires throughout the dungeon rooms, and she handed him one. He slipped on the garment and tied the sash. *Ah well, so much for secrets.* He supposed his mother's support would be better than her finding out once it was all said and done.

Trudy opened her mouth, then snapped it closed. She scrunched her eyes in confusion before she spoke. "And what is she doing here?"

Kit snuggled into his side. "We should tell her."

"Tell me what?" Trudy's expression wavered between annoyance and hurt.

Kat and Evan had exited the car by this point and were walking arm in arm into the barn. Tossing her red hair over her shoulder, Kat called out, "The gang's all here!"

"I didn't realize it was clothing optional," Evan remarked, glancing down at his jeans and t-shirt. He ran a hand over his close-cropped dark hair. "I feel over-dressed."

"Me too." Kat swished her green skirt from side to side.

Greg rolled his eyes and shook his head.

"Would somebody please explain?" Trudy placed her hands on her hips again.

Greg held out a hand to her. "Come on, Mom, I'll show you."

Trudy walked toward him but deliberately held her hands out in front of her. "Thanks, but I don't know where your hands have been."

Greg winked at Kit. "That is a fair assumption."

Trudy gave him the side-eye. "So, it worked? I fixed you two up after all?"

Kit laced her arm through his. "You got us talking again, but we had fixed ourselves up already." She glanced over her shoulder at Evan and Kat. "You two coming?"

"Not coming yet," Evan grinned. "But if you mean to follow you, then yes, because I'm not missing out on this show."

"Me either," Kat agreed with a mischievous smile on her face.

"So, what is it the two of you have to show me?" Trudy asked.

Greg opened the door for his mother to enter first. "Welcome to Country Kink."

Trudy raised an eyebrow, then hesitantly stepped over the threshold. Greg watched his mother as her gaze swept the room. Her loud gasp echoed about the silent space as he and the others waited for her to express her reaction.

He and Kit had converted one half of the barn into an open playroom where people could gather for workshops or parties. St. Andrews crosses on wheels were stationed at the far end of the space, ready to be rolled out and locked into position where needed.

Multiple hooks and riggings hung from the ceiling for people to practice rope play in the center of the room. Cabinets were attached to the wall at intervals filled with toys of various kinds. They contained everything from ropes, other types of restraints, dildos, vibrators, and every lube imaginable. Horses, Sybians, and wooden platforms—all homemade by Greg—were set along the other two walls, and they could be moved to any position in the room.

At the far end, the cellar doors led down into a dungeon where he and Kit had created four private rooms. Each had its own toilet and shower. All of it had been a labour of love over the past five years, and with Kit's help and vision in the last couple of months, the creative process had gone even smoother.

Proud, to say the least, Greg's heart filled with joy at what they had created. He squeezed Kit to his side and bestowed a kiss to the top of her head.

Trudy finished looking around the room, glanced at Greg, but didn't say a word. She walked over to one of the cabinets and opened the door, then did the same to all of them, touching the horses and contraptions along the way. When she'd finished touring the room, she came to stand in front of him.

He and his mother stared each other square in the eye, neither speaking for a moment. Kit snaked an arm around his waist in support. Trudy's gaze bounced between the two of them, but she still hadn't said a word.

Greg mused that this was the longest period of silence he'd ever experienced with his mother.

Trudy narrowed her eyes at him for a moment, then her gaze softened, and he swore she began to tear up. Before a tear could be shed, she took a deep breath, and whatever emotion had begun to surface disappeared before it could be expressed.

If he wasn't mistaken, understanding flashed through his mother's eyes. She nodded at him, then indicated the room. "You're a kinky fucker, aren't ya?"

Greg barked a laugh. "Yeah, Mom, I am."

"Well, why didn't ya ever say anything?" Trudy shook her head. "Kids," she muttered, "they always think they're the first to try kinky stuff . . ."

Greg felt Kit press her face into his upper arm, attempting to stifle a giggle. Dumbfounded, Greg asked, "So, you're not surprised?"

Trudy shrugged a shoulder. "I'm not surprised you have kinky inclinations. I am surprised that you've done all this renovating right under my nose without me knowing."

Greg rolled his eyes. "Mom, you've been having a good time since you moved out, and it's not like I've ever told you my plans for my life."

"I know." A grumpy expression took up residence on her face, and she crossed her arms over her chest. "Why do you think I agreed to let your father be the go-between? At least then I had some clue. You were a talkative kid and told me everything until you were about ten years old. Then you just . . . stopped. I felt like a failure as a mother when I couldn't get you to talk with me anymore."

Greg squeezed Kit, released her, then took hold of his mother's shoulders. He ducked his head so he could look her in the eye. "Do you know what happened when I was ten?"

Trudy's eyebrows pinched together in a frown. "I cannot recall anything happening to you at that age. If it was with your friends, you would have told me. It was like a switch flipped, and you became a different person."

Greg hung his head and decided it was time to tell his mother the truth. He released a sigh. "Remember Susie McNeil?"

"Yeah, little Susie," his mom said. "She always had those blonde pigtails and was as cute as a button. Isn't she married to that Matt guy now?"

Greg smiled. "Actually, they're engaged. And they're our first customer. They've decided to hold their wedding here."

"Wow, you have been busy," Trudy commented. "You're open for business already. Anyway, what about little Susie?"

Greg scratched the top of his head. "I liked her when I was ten."

"Oh, that's right," Trudy exclaimed. "You did. You went on and on about how cute she was and how much you liked her . . ." Her face fell. "Wait a minute . . . why did you stop talking about her? Was she mean to you? Oh, her mother could be a right old bitch sometimes—"

"No, Mom. Nothing like that." Greg cleared his throat. "Well, one day I came inside from playing out in the field. I had picked this great bouquet of wildflowers, and I was going to ask you if I should be brave and give them to her."

"I don't recall you saying anything to me," Trudy said. "What happened?"

"You're right. I didn't say a word. Dad thought it would be a great idea, so I came inside to ask you. I valued your opinion, you know. I loved that you had an opinion on anything and everything and seemed so sure of yourself." Greg straightened up and dropped his hands away from her shoulders. "When I came inside, you were talking on the phone with Mavis."

"And?" Trudy prompted.

"And I overheard your conversation." His cheeks heated, and he shifted as the uncomfortable memory surfaced. "You were telling Mavis how Dad had tied you up the night before and being helpless had been such a great addition to your sex life. I was intrigued, titillated by the conversation if you will. It excited me in a way to hear you talking about sex."

Trudy glared at him. "You shouldn't have been eavesdropping."

"It isn't like you were ever quiet with what you talked about, Mom. Gossiping was your game."

"It is not," Trudy protested.

Greg turned around to enlist Kit, Kat, and Evan's support. All three of them lifted their hands in surrender and looked anywhere but at Trudy or him. "Thanks, guys." He turned his attention back to Trudy. "I was ten years old, hearing my mother talk about sex. No, I shouldn't have been eavesdropping, but are you telling me you've never done that?"

"I won't lie. I've eavesdropped many a time. Get the best goss—er, news that way," she conceded. "But that was a private conversation, and one you should never have heard. Are you saying it scarred you for life?"

"Not exactly, but I did hear it, and I wanted to ask you a million questions."

Trudy scuffed the toe of her boot against the ground. "I would have talked to you about anything."

"I know," Greg admitted. "But then I heard you mention to Mavis how cute it was that I had a crush on Susie, and I realized that not only did you make your business everyone else's business, but you were making my business everyone's business."

"That's what mothers do!" Trudy massaged her forehead. "I was telling my best friend about something that was important to you because you're my son and I was happy for you. That's not gossip . . . it's bragging."

"Well, at the impressionable age of ten, it didn't feel like bragging, and I thought that if you couldn't keep that a secret, then I shouldn't tell you anything else. And I didn't." Greg rocked back on his heels, waiting for her reaction.

"But . . . We . . . All this time . . ." She spluttered several attempts at a reply. "I need to sit down."

Kit hurried to get one of the chairs from along one wall. She slid it under Trudy as the woman plopped down.

Trudy placed her elbows on her knees and propped her head in her hands. "Wow. I am the worst mother ever."

Greg knelt in front of her. "You're not the worst mother. You've been a good mom. You've supported me and let me have the relationship with Dad. You accepted that I'd rather talk to him, even though you'd rather have been the one in the know."

"Yeah, I suppose." She lifted her head. "How did I not know you were eavesdropping? You were a sneaky little bugger."

Greg chuckled. "Yeah, that I was. I went back outside and

told Dad what I overheard. He was kind of uncomfortable with the conversation, but he explained how people experimented with sex. Dad always answered my questions and supported me in exploring. He told me to give Susie the flowers and see what happened."

"What did happen?" Trudy asked.

He shrugged. "She told me she had a crush on someone else and that she'd marry him someday. And she is." He took Kit's hand in his. "It hasn't mattered for a long time, but I'm happy I have my own special someone."

Kit squeezed his hand. "We are good for each other."

Greg smiled at Kit. "Agreed."

Trudy smiled, then took hold of Kit's free hand and cupped Greg's cheek. "I'm glad you have someone, son. It's all I wanted for you. And if you had told me that you didn't want me to tell your business to other people, I would have listened."

Greg took her hand in his. "Really?"

They stared at each other for a second, before Trudy sighed. "Well, I would have listened, and tried very hard not to, but you were so damned cute and I was so proud of you, that I wanted everyone to know every damn thing about you."

Greg hung his head for a second, then chuckled, unable to help himself. "That's what I thought."

Trudy held her arms up with a shrug. "I like to talk, son. Not gonna lie. The whole town probably would have known everything about you, instead of hearing me complain about how I knew nothing."

Greg shook his head and stood. "Well, what are you going to tell them now?"

Trudy tugged on his hand and stood up, too. "Am I supposed to keep this a secret? Is this for fun or a business?"

Greg grinned. "Both. Kit and I want to hold conferences,

workshops, parties here for people to explore the kinkier side of their sexuality. We're hoping that Country Kink Bed and Breakfast will take off."

Evan and Kat who had been silent until now spoke up.

"You know what they say . . . *if you build it, they will come,*" Kat quipped.

"Quite literally is the hope, it seems," Evan added. "I'm happy for you, man. If there's anything we can do to make it a success, you can count us in. The space looks great, and I can't wait to see the rest of it."

"And me too," Trudy interjected. "I know a few people at the senior's home who might be interested."

Kit put in her two cents. "We would appreciate any help we can get. Which reminds me . . ." She walked toward a table at the entrance, opened a drawer, and took out a few sheets of paper along with a couple of pens. "We have confidentiality agreements, and we'd like you all to sign."

Without question, Kat and Evan walked over to the table to peruse the document.

"So, what, we can't talk about this place? How do we get the word out?" Trudy asked as she walked toward the table.

"It's not that you can't talk about it," Kit said. "It's an agreement that what happens at Country Kink stays at Country Kink. You can tell people you had a good time, or make recommendations, but you cannot divulge any specific details of your stay on social media or blog without permission, or we will sue the fucking pants off you."

"Well, I suppose that makes sense," Trudy muttered as she took her turn to read a document. "Did you ask little Davie Huett to look it over? I heard he's a big-time lawyer now."

"Actually, yeah, we did. *David,*" Greg emphasized the name, "was a fantastic help, and very supportive. I feel we've covered all our bases." He took Kit into his arms again, feeling a sense of peace inside he hadn't felt since being a child.

To his surprise, Trudy signed on the spot with a flourish worthy of an award-winning performance. Then she put her hands on her hips and squared off with Greg. "You know, if you had talked to me earlier, we might have been able to put this behind us sooner."

Greg shrugged. "But we didn't. And I'll admit that since I was a child, I told myself over and over that I couldn't trust you with my secrets. I will own that, and if it has hurt you, I'm sorry."

Trudy dropped her hands, then fiddled with them, seeming unsure of what to do with herself. "Well, I'm sorry you overheard that conversation at such a young age. I'm glad it didn't scar you for life. I'll take it as a win that you chose to explore what you were curious about."

Greg walked over to her and wrapped her in a hug. "I love you, Mom."

"I love you, too, son." Trudy looked up into his face. "And I'm proud of the man you've become."

Tears welled up in both of their eyes, and Greg continued to stare at her. Trudy broke the moment by stepping back, wiping her hands down her slacks, and then clapping her hands together.

"Well, don't let me keep you kids from having fun," Trudy said. "I'm going to see if I can convince George to step it up a notch and visit here with me." Greg opened his mouth to protest, but she waved away his complaint. "I'll see ya later. Toodles!"

His mother turned and marched out of the barn. Greg watched from the doorway as she walked through the main hall and out to her car. Once the sound of the engine reached his ears, he turned his attention back to Kit and their friends.

Greg scratched his head. "I'll admit I was hoping we'd see less of her if we were honest about what we did out here."

"For what it's worth, I think it's great you told your mom

what you're into," Kat said. "She'd probably find out anyway and be less hurt hearing it from you. In fact, she seems quite supportive."

"Yeah," Evan chimed in. "Plus, you can charge her full price for use of any of the rooms."

Kit held out her arms to him. "Face it, honey, you got your kinky inclinations from someone, and it turns out it was your parents. Embrace it. It will be much easier."

Greg snorted. "I'm not in the mood for therapy."

She raised an eyebrow at him. "That sounds kind of bratty to me. Is a punishment in order?"

Feeling happier and more playful than he had in a long time, he quirked one corner of his mouth in a smile. "What do you have in mind?"

CHAPTER FIVE

"Wow." Greg wriggled in his restraints, hands tied behind his back, secured to ropes that bound his ankles together while he sat in a kneeling position on the floor. "This isn't quite what I had in mind."

"I didn't hear you object." Kit winked at him. "Besides, I know how much you like being the voyeur. Consider yourself a captive one this time. If you sincerely object, now is the time to say so."

Greg glanced over at Evan. "You're okay with me watching?"

Evan shrugged. "Whenever I'm curious, I try something at least once. I'm actually more worried about you being upset that I'm playing with your woman."

"Mistress," Greg corrected before Kit had a chance to respond. "In this situation, she's my Mistress. And what she says goes."

Kit beamed at him, then came over to tug on the ropes to make sure they were tight. Her lips hovered over his. "They're not cutting off any circulation?"

Greg shook his head. "Feels great, Mistress."

Kit grasped his chin in her hand. "This is the time to say if you're not comfortable."

Greg puckered his lips, and she indulged him in a quick peck on the lips. "Mistress, I have no objections."

Kit released him. "Then enjoy. And remember, no coming until I give you permission."

"Yes, Mistress."

Greg's cock hardened at the sight of her ass as she walked away. Kit wore thigh-high boots, a thong, a bustier that made her nipples protrude, and sported a riding crop in one hand, all in black. He loved the round shape of her ass and the sway of her hips as she strode over to where Kat had been tied to a St. Andrew's cross a few feet away from where he knelt.

Kat's long red hair cascaded over her shoulders, her head resting against the leather cushion attached to the cross for comfort. She wore a lacy pink bra and underwear, and she squirmed under everyone's scrutiny.

The entire scene made Greg want to come. He concentrated on his breathing, willing his body to relax, yet maintain a state of arousal. He'd watched a lot of BDSM porn over the years and had observed such scenes while away at conventions, but he knew this moment was special. He was sharing his most vulnerable secret, not only with the woman he loved, but also two of his closest friends, and he felt no judgment from anyone.

A lump of emotion formed in his throat. He chose to go over some facts in his mind to keep himself from becoming too emotional before they'd even started.

Kat and Kit were best friends and lovers on occasion. Greg had been friends with Evan for many years. Evan, as the local vet, took care of the animals on the farm. He'd been one of the first guy friends Greg had told about his kinky inclinations. Evan had always accepted Greg for who he was, asking questions out of curiosity and to understand, never to judge. Evan and Kat had been together for a few months now, ever since a romantic date had gone to shit — quite literally — when one of the horses Evan had rented from him for a carriage ride had refused to do anything due to intestinal issues. Quirky and fun, Kat was good for Evan, and Greg couldn't have been happier for his friend.

Greg felt honoured he could share this time with all the people he cared about most in the world. With Kit, he knew he would be safe to explore all the kinky things he could envision.

The sound of the riding crop smacking against the wood of the cross brought Greg back to the present.

"Are you paying attention, slut?" Kit asked.

"Yes, Ma'am." Greg concentrated on the scene before him.

Evan had removed his shirt and jeans and stood beside Kat. "So, what do I do?"

Kit began tapping the riding crop on Kat's pussy on the outside of her underwear. Kat moaned and squirmed in the restraints.

"Play with her breasts," Kit instructed Evan.

Evan cupped and squeezed Kat's tits. He nuzzled her arms, placing kisses on her skin. Greg watched as Kat's eyes rolled back in her head. He understood what it meant to be helpless that way, and the pleasure experienced in such a situation.

Evan pulled Kat's bra aside and took turns licking each of her nipples. He nibbled her flesh while Kit kept tapping her cunt with the riding crop. Kat's moans turned to loud groans as she surrendered to the moment.

The scene before him caused Greg's cock to harden to the point of painful. He loved being forced to watch Kit dominate another person, imagining himself in the scenario. It turned him on in a way he'd only imagined, and he realized imagination had nothing on the real thing.

"Finger her pussy," Kit instructed Evan. She pulled Kit's bra straps down her shoulders, exposing her breasts to the air. Her nipples hardened, and the sight made Greg moan.

Evan pulled aside Kat's underwear and toyed with her clit. Kat tried to squirm but to no avail. He pushed two fingers inside her cunt, while Kit tapped the riding crop against her taut nipples. Kat's moans turned to squeals with every tap against her tits. Evan thrust his fingers in and out of her in a slow rhythm.

"Eat her," Kit commanded.

Evan dropped to his knees in compliance. He buried his

face in her pussy while continuing to pump his fingers in and out of her. Kat's eyes bugged out of her head, her squeals getting louder. Kit grabbed both of her breasts and squeezed, then suckled each nipple in turn. Kat's head rolled from side to side, then she let out a shriek, her body straining against her bonds.

Watching her orgasm nearly sent Greg over the edge. He groaned, tensing all his muscles to prevent release.

"Oh, please, let me down," Kat begged. "Please . . ."

"Of course, sweetie," Kit assured her. "Help me untie her, Evan."

Evan wiped pussy juice off his mouth with the back of his hand, then assisted Kit. "That was so hot, honey." He pressed a kiss to Kat's mouth.

"Thanks," she gasped. "It was very intense. I need to process."

"Why don't the two of you go into one of the dungeon rooms? You'll have privacy to play some more, or shower and cuddle if you like," Kit suggested. "Let me know if you need anything."

They helped Kat to her feet, then Evan scooped her into his arms. "Sounds great." With that, he carried Kat over to the cellar, and Kit followed to open the door for them.

Greg watched his friends disappear down the stairs. His feet had begun to tingle, a sign he had restricted blood flow. "Mistress?"

"Yes, slut?" Kit hurried over to him and cupped his face in her hands. "Your feet are falling asleep, aren't they?"

"Yes, Mistress."

Kit remedied the situation quickly, helping him to his feet. Greg shook out his legs and wriggled his torso while his hands remained tied behind his back.

"Did you enjoy that?" she asked.

"Very much, Mistress."

Kit smiled and traced his jaw with her fingertip. "Whatever shall I do with you, my pet?"

Greg grinned. "Whatever you wish, Mistress."

Kit couldn't help the grin that took over her face. She'd shared an incredible scene with people who meant the most to her, and she was about to be even more intimate with the man she loved.

Then it hit her—he'd told her earlier how he felt, but she hadn't had a chance to reciprocate. He hadn't seemed bothered by it, but then again, she'd taken his grim demeanour to mean that he'd been annoyed by the unexpected visit from his mother.

The man standing before her had gifted her with his submission. He respected her as a lover and business partner and wanted to help her dreams come true. He accepted her lifestyle, wanted to be part of it, and committed to building a business and a life with her. She couldn't get any luckier than that.

And he deserved the teasing of his life along with her love.

"Sit down on that bench over there, slut," she instructed.

"Yes, Mistress." Greg complied with her request and sat on the end of the bench with his legs together.

"Spread your legs," she commanded.

He obeyed, and Kit knelt between his thighs. "No coming until I say."

"Yes, Mistress."

His breathless voice turned her on. Her cunt ached to have him inside her. But first, she wanted to torture him to the brink of release before she took her pleasure, leaving him shaking and begging for more.

Kit dipped her head and nuzzled his cock and balls, inhaling the scent of him. With the tip of her tongue, she drew a line up the length of his cock. With both hands, she stroked him, while at the same time swirling her tongue around the plump crown of the head.

Greg's leg muscles tensed at her ministrations, and Kit sensed his struggle to remain still. She bobbed up and down, swallowing his length over and over, deep throating him. She loved giving head, and only did so within the boundaries of a loving relationship, never in her work life as a Domme. This simple pleasure gave her as much joy as if she were on the receiving end of it. The thin material of her thong was soaked from her dripping cunt, and she couldn't wait to take her pleasure by riding his long, hard cock. But she waited, teasing Greg more with her mouth, tongue, and hands.

When he groaned in earnest, she couldn't wait any longer. Kit stood up and straddled his lap, holding onto his shoulders for support. She positioned his cock outside her pussy, then slowly lowered herself onto his length. She groaned out loud when she fully engulfed him, loving the way his cock filled her.

Kit ground down onto him, braced her feet against the floor, then began to ride him. She bounced up and down, driving his cock into her cunt. They stared into each other's eyes. Her fingernails dug into his shoulders as her orgasm built, but she could tell he remained in control as she'd told him to.

"Come with me," she commanded.

Greg's eyes rolled back in his head. "Yes, Mistress."

Each time she dropped down onto his length, he let out a grunt. Soon the sound of their harsh panting and groaning filled the room.

Kit's head dropped back, and she squeezed her eyes shut tight as her orgasm rocked through her.

Greg ground out, "I'm gonna come . . ."

Kit lifted herself off his cock, and Greg came against her

stomach.

For a moment, Kit felt suspended in time, floating on a high she'd only imagined could occur for two people. Then she realized she was floating . . . or rather falling backward off his lap.

She gripped his shoulders tight, trying to keep herself upright, her legs scrabbling for purchase against the floor. They'd purposely used rubber grip flooring to prevent slips and spills when people played here, but it didn't seem to be helping at this point. She was going down, and with his hands tied behind his back, Greg had no way to help her.

Kit hit the floor with a loud *oof*. She blinked the stars from her eyes. Other than winding herself, she didn't feel hurt anywhere.

Greg's eyes widened in shock. "Oh my God! Are you okay?"

For a moment, Kit couldn't speak. Then giggles erupted. They'd certainly finished with a bang. "Yeah, I'm all right," she managed to wheeze out.

"Are you able to untie me?" he asked, concern for her well-being etched all over his face.

Kit rolled to her side and pushed herself into a sitting position. Cum dribbled off her belly, and she laughed some more.

"What is it?" Greg asked.

She glanced over at him. "This is the un-sexiest thing that's ever happened to me."

He grinned. "You still look sexy and dominating as hell to me."

Kit got onto her hands and knees and crawled to Greg. "I don't appear to be broken." She paused to rub her back and indulge in a groan. Then she went to work untying his arms, rubbing some circulation back into his limbs as she did. "You okay?"

Once freed, Greg shook out his arms, then wrapped her in a hug. "I'm not the only one who needs aftercare."

She shrugged a shoulder. "I could use a little TLC."

He pressed a hard kiss to her lips, then stood and assisted her onto the bench. "Wait here." He fetched her robe where she'd dropped it before playtime began. He draped it around her shoulders, waiting until she slipped her arms into the sleeves. Then he offered a hand to help her stand up.

Kit took the offered hand and snuggled into him as she stood. He wrapped her in his arms. "If I may make a suggestion, Mistress."

She released a sigh. "Yes, please."

"Let's have a long, hot bath together," he suggested. "Then we make some food, cuddle, and talk through all of the emotions we are processing. I'm not sure about you, but I need it."

"You do?" Kit looked into his eyes. "I would love that."

"Good. I'm glad I found someone I can communicate with that I trust." Greg kissed the top of her head, released her from the embrace, then started toward the exit.

"Wait." Kit couldn't go on about their day if she didn't tell him how she felt about him. He deserved to know.

"What is it?" he asked when she didn't take his hand.

"Earlier, I didn't get a chance to respond to what you said to me." She swallowed hard as emotions filled her heart.

"What did I say?" His eyebrows furrowed in question.

Kit cleared her throat, her cheeks heating. "Well, I hope you remember when I tell you, because this could be awkward."

Greg's cheeks reddened, and he shuffled his feet. "I told you I loved you."

Kit took his face in her hands. "I love you, too. So much. I don't even have words to describe how much I appreciate your presence in my life."

His mouth twitched with a boyish grin. "I . . . I don't know what to say to that."

"You don't have to say anything." She pressed a soft kiss to his lips. "You allow me to be who I am, you accept my jobs, and you want to work with me to provide safe spaces for people to explore their sexuality . . . I could go on, but the bottom line is that you're amazing, Greg. There is no one else I want to build a life with. And I love you."

Greg snaked his arms around her waist. "There is no one I want to build a life with more than you. Everything you said about me, applies to how I feel about you too. I'm glad one of us can express themselves with words. You're so much better at it than I am."

She tapped his nose with a fingertip. "You need more practice, that's all. So many years of not trusting your mother, you're bound to have a few issues."

He stuck his tongue out at her. "Apparently." He scooped her up into his arms. "So, counsellor, want to counsel me and help me move through my *mommy* issues?"

Kit looped her arms around his neck and shook her head. "No, not really," she teased. "I'm kind of tired at the moment, but if you want to talk about anything, I'm always here to listen."

"Awesome." He started toward the door. "I'm glad to hear you won't be bugging me to talk about my feelings all the time." He stopped short. "Damn, I'm not wearing any pants."

"It's only a short walk to the house." She couldn't hold back her laugh.

"Yeah, but with my luck, the whole damn town will be outside."

"One day they might be. I mean, we just told your mom the kind of business we are building. She's not going to keep quiet about it, and I bet some of the first customers are ones she procures."

Greg shouldered the door open. "That is probably true."

"As long as little Susie doesn't want a piece of you, I'm okay with it." Kit winked to show she teased.

Greg grimaced. "Little Susie is definitely not my type. Word is, she might be more your type."

"Oh, do tell."

"That's a story for another time. I love you, Kit. And I'm only sharing you with people we agree on."

"Ditto." She puckered her lips and leaned in to kiss him. "I love you, too. Now that I've roped my rancher, there's nowhere I'd rather be."

The End

Excerpt

Oh, great line. Madison swallowed the saliva pooling in her mouth from sneaking a peek at Marnie's cleavage. Since the day Marnie had brought them cake, all she'd been able to think about was interesting places to eat cake off of Marnie's body. She loved Drake with all her heart, but as a bisexual female, there was something special about being with a woman, and she missed it.

Since she and Marnie had only spoken a handful of words, she couldn't explain the fierce attraction she had for the green-eyed brunette. She cleared her throat, hoping to rid her head of dirty thoughts at the same time. Lifting her chin to indicate Marnie's attire, she said, "I hope I'm not interrupting anything."

"Nope. Not really. Just me. Home. Alone. On a Friday night." Marnie's cheeks coloured.

So cute! But why would she be embarrassed to be caught at home alone? Unless she's done something naughty. Madison liked naughty. Inhaling, she caught a whiff of pussy. As the delicious scent permeated her senses, a jolt of desire slashed through her abdomen and travelled straight to her cunt.

What am I doing? Her desire for her new neighbour

overrode common sense. She had to find out first if Marnie was even into women, never mind a threesome between her and her boyfriend. One thing at a time.

Drake had embraced Madison's bisexuality with enthusiasm, telling her that any time she found a woman she wanted to fuck, he'd be there. What more could a woman ask for?

A woman. This woman in front of me. Deep in her gut, she knew her sexy neighbour could make everything complete. But, even if Marnie happened to be into women, that didn't mean she'd be into men, too.

Marnie folded her arms across her chest, squishing her tits together. The sight made Madison's mouth water all over again.

"So . . . You really need to borrow some sugar?" Marnie asked.

"Um . . . Yeesss . . ."

Marnie raised an eyebrow, but stepped aside to let Madison enter. "Sugar?"

"Yes, sugar." As Madison entered the apartment, her arm grazed Marnie's breast through the fabric of the robe. The distinct scent of pussy grew stronger, and Madison couldn't stand it any longer. It would be a bold move but her brain insisted she get right to the point.

As Marnie shut the door, Madison blocked her, forcing the brunette against the door. Green eyes widened with surprise as Madison stepped into her personal space, leaving only centimetres separating them. "I sure hope you have some sugar for me." Her voice came out a sexy purr.

Marnie's brows scrunched together in confusion. "What do you mean exactly?"

Courage faltering, she cleared her throat. Just go for it. Madison inhaled deep through her nose and closed her eyes for a second, letting the scent of pussy fill her senses once more. Her eyes popped open, her gaze boring holes into green sparkly ones. "Are you busy tonight?"

Marnie wiggled in a nervous gesture under Madison's intense stare. "Um, no . . . Why?"

"I want to crash your party for one." Madison could tell she'd taken Marnie completely by surprise. Damn. At that moment, she wanted to slap herself. I'm coming on too strong. Whatever happened to "Hi, how are you? Nice weather we're having . . ." Oh no, she just came out and embarrassed the one woman who had haunted her sexual thoughts for a few weeks now.

Oh, well. In for a penny as they say. "I've wanted you since the first time I saw you," she blurted, placing her hands on the door on either side of Marnie's head.

Marnie's eyes popped open wide in disbelief. "Really?"

"Yes, really." Madison hung her head and raked a hand through her hair. "Sorry! God, I've messed this up."

"You . . . are direct. More than I have been."

"It's a bad habit," she admitted, tone sheepish. "Wait—what did you say?"

"You are far more direct than me." The blush on Marnie's cheeks deepened.

"You mean you want my sugar?" Madison asked.

"Well, I did bring you a cake." A small smile crinkled at the corners of Marnie's mouth.

Madison grinned. "And it was good cake, too."

Marnie giggled. "Believe me, if you knew my family, this isn't the worst way anyone has been direct about anything."

The two women stared at each other.

Madison spoke first. "So."

"So."

Madison drew a few strands of Marnie's hair down between her fingers. "Soft, like I'd imagined."

"You've really thought about me?" Marnie questioned.

"Yeah. A lot." Madison sighed. She'd fantasized about Marnie between her legs even when Drake was getting her off.

"I've thought about you too." Marnie's Adam's apple

bobbed when she swallowed hard.

Hope filled Madison's chest. "Yeah?"

"Uh-huh. But I thought you were straight. I mean, I hear you and Drake going at it like night and day. Uh, not that I'm, you know, trying to hear you or anything . . ."

Is that longing I hear in her voice? Madison grinned. It would be a lot easier if all three of them were attracted to each other. Madison already knew Drake thought Marnie was hot, even though he was in love with her. When Madison told him she wanted to go after their neighbour, he'd told her to go for it. Would Madison get her wish—to have both cock and pussy at the same time?

First things first. She wanted Marnie alone for the first time, giving her the opportunity to explore, get to know her, what she liked, what made her squirm, what made her pussy clench in the throes of an orgasm.

"I'm a lucky woman. Drake loves me, is very adventurous in the bedroom, and embraces my bisexual nature. But we haven't found a woman yet to fulfill that fantasy."

"Oh, so it's a fantasy you're looking to fulfill."

Madison registered the crushed look on Marnie's face. "Well, it's not just a fantasy . . . It's just . . . Well, I . . . I want to . . ." As direct as she could be, there were times she didn't know how to woo anyone. "I'm totally messing this up."

Marnie smiled, the joy not quite reaching her eyes. Regardless, she tucked a red lock of hair back behind Madison's ear. "Maybe we should get to know each other a little better."

Madison shivered at the touch. "Just what I had in mind." She knew precisely how well she wanted to get to know Marnie. "Where should we start?" she asked, trying not to sound too eager, or fuck up her intentions any more than she already had.

"Let's start with that sugar." With that statement, Marnie cupped the back of Madison's neck and smothered her lips in a kiss.

About the Author

Winner of the RONE (Reward of Novel Excellence) Award for Best Erotica 2012, Kellie Kamryn has many 5-star reviews from sites such as Night Owl Reviews for her work in contemporary romantic fiction. In 2013, one of her novellas was nominated for Best Novella for the RONE Awards. In addition, she is an online columnist and workshop presenter.

All of Kellie's books contain a lot of heat balanced with an abundance of Heart. With twenty-five books and two anthologies to her credit, her creative talents also include, producing and narrating audiobooks and scriptwriting.

As a lifelong physical educator, she has trained competitive gymnasts, coaches, and spends some of her time co-teaching the martial art of Baguazhang as a method of health and self-defence to women, families, and individuals on the autism spectrum.

Visit with her at: www.kelliekamryn.com